PLANETOID DISPOSALS LTD.

PLANETOID DISPOSALS LTD.

E.C. TUBB

WILDSIDE PRESS

CHAPTER ONE

A thin bright streak lanced across the midnight sky—a slender thread of almost unbearable brilliance, swift, and dying as it neared the horizon. It was followed by another, and yet another, and for a moment the dark sweep of the heavens seemed to be laced with the burning threads of dying meteors plunging towards Earth.

Dell Franson stared at them, his hard young features tightening and his cold grey eyes glittering as if they were carved of some ancient stone. "The Leonids, and earlier than usual."

"Does it matter?"

"You ask that?" Dell sighed and turned away from the window. He stared at his companion, a small shrewd-eyed man with thinning hair and the lines of age graven deep into his leather skin.

"You of all people should know what it could mean." Dell turned back to the window and pointed to where the thin trails still lanced across the sky. "Out there, space is lousy with a million shattered pieces of some broken world. Splinters of stone and jagged iron, some a few grains in weight, others several tons, but each and every piece a potential menace."

"What can we do about it?"

"A lot, Jeff, quite a lot." He glanced at the watch strapped to his wrist and frowned. "When did Harmond say that he'd be here?"

"As soon as he could get away from the conference. You know how it is at this time of the year, all the owners are worried sick at what may happen to their ships."

"I can understand that." Dell smiled a little as he stared out of the window. "Spaceships cost money, lots of money and it would take just a few ounces of rock to turn the biggest of them into worthless junk. A meteor, a scrap of stone or metal travelling on a collision orbit with a spaceship, and anything could happen. The best they could hope for is to scar the hull, perhaps a minor puncture easily repaired, but it could be worse, lots worse."

"You don't have to tell me." The old man wriggled on his chair. "I know what could happen—it did! I was chief pilot remember on the *Vesta*, and I was one of the seven survivors out of two hundred and thirty passengers and crew. The meteor which struck us couldn't have been more than a couple of hundred-weight, but its velocity was such that it volatised into incandescent gas on impact. What was left of the *Vesta* wasn't worth salvaging."

The humming attention call from the intercom interrupted Dell's reply and eagerly he closed the circuit. "Yes?"

"Mr. Harmond is here, sir."

"Good. Ask him to come right up, will you."

He opened the circuit and turned to the old man. "He's here, now you know what to do, Jeff."

"Yes, but aren't you relying on me a little too much? Remember that Harmond blames me for the loss of the *Vesta*, he's not going to take much notice of what I say."

"Never mind, just do as I told you." Dell forced a smile to his lips as the door swung open.

Harmond was a big man, big in every sense of the word. His great bulk strained at the seams of his blouse, and yet he was not fat, his bulk came from bone and muscle. He stood and looked at Dell for a moment, then his eyes slid from the hard features of the young man to the shrewd eyes of the old one. He grinned. "A nice looking pair," he grunted, "am I to be the pigeon?"

"If that's what you are thinking Harmond, perhaps you'd better leave now!"

"Steady!" Jeff frowned at Dell then smiled at the big man standing just within the room. "Sit down, Mr. Harmond, my friend here has a proposition which should interest you quite a lot."

"It had better be good, I've come a long way to this meeting, and I'm still wondering just why I've come at all."

"I know why you're here, Harmond." Dell slid into a chair and gestured for the big man to be seated. "How much does it cost you for each day your ships are grounded?"

"A lot, why?"

"The Leonids are early this year, you daren't take any chances and that means that your ships must either stay grounded, or if they are in flight, must stay clear of the meteor stream. That means fuel, food, and extra water. That means idle ships and crews who still must be paid. It means timid passengers and liability for undelivered cargo. It means money, Harmond, lots of money."

"Well?"

"I can save you all that money, all the delay, all the bad feeling. That's why you've come here, because you are interested enough to hear what I have to say, and more than half-willing to agree with what I propose."

"Am I?" Harmond smiled and slowly took a cigar from an inner pocket. Deliberately he clipped the end and rolled it between his fingers as he stared at the young man seated across the wide desk.

"Yes."

"I wonder?" Harmond lit the cigar, the thick blue smoke coiling and writhing as he gestured with his hand. "I know you, Franson, and I think I know what you're going to propose, but I've heard it all before and my answer is still the same."

"Is it?" Dell smiled and leaned across the table. "What do you think I'm going to ask you for, Harmond?"

"Money, lots of it, and for it you will promise an impossible dream."

"Am I?"

"I told you that I've heard it all before, and nice as it sounds, it will never work. Space is too big, too vast for any fleet of ships, no matter how large, to sweep away the debris." The big man drew deeply on his cigar. "No, Dell. You can never sweep space clean of meteors, neither you nor any other man."

"I don't intend to."

"What?"

"No, I'm no starry-eyed dreamer, I know space and the conditions out there as well as any man, we could never do as you suggest, but why should we?"

"I don't understand. What else have you to offer?"

"That's my secret, but I'll tell you this, Harmond, what I have in mind will work!"

"I see." Deliberately the big man crushed out his cigar. "Perhaps you'd better tell me about it."

"Fundamentally it is simple. You don't ground your ships all the time, only when meteor showers such as the Leonids are due, the rest of the time you take a chance, and the odds are in your favour. The chance of a big meteorite hitting a spaceship is very remote, but that's not what I'm interested in."

"No?"

"No, that can be part of it of course. I know how to deflect the stream so that it will strike the sun and be destroyed; within a few years the Leonids will be a thing of the past." Dell glanced at Jeff, and then at the big man. "I have a plan, and I know that it will work. A simple plan, really, but like most simple things, utterly effective."

"Yes?"

"You are a businessman, Harmond, what would you say to a proposition like this? Unlimited quantities of iron, copper, tungsten, and the heavy elements, all free, all costing no more than freight and mining costs, all just waiting to be picked up?"

"Are you serious?"

"Wait a moment, I haven't finished yet. What would you say to new worlds, entire planets to be sold to the highest bidder, all warm and green and lovely? Think of it, Harmond! Entire planetoids for sale! Masses of readily available minerals, all just waiting for someone to step in, and pick them up."

"I see!" The big man stared at Dell. "The Asteroids!"

"Yes."

"You surprise me, for a moment I had thought that you had something really worthwhile to offer me, but the Asteroids!"

"You don't think that what I suggest is possible."

"No."

"Why not?"

"Isn't it simple? You plan to operate the Asteroid Belt, mining where you can, and for the other things, I'll be generous and stay silent. Think of it for moment, Dell. You'd have to transport every little thing you needed, and even from Mars that would mean quite a haul. You'd have to set up a refining plant, opencast workings, living quarters…a dozen things not always possible even on Earth. The cost of freight from the Belt would be fantastic, and that's not even thinking about the cost of labour, mining plant, and transport to the workings. No, the idea isn't new but tempting as it sounds, it won't stand a second thought."

"I agree with you, but for one thing."

"And that is?"

"Tell him, Jeff."

"Jeff?" Harmond swung round in his chair and glared at the old man. "What does he know about it? An ex-chief pilot who lost his ship?"

The old man flushed and bit his lips his thin old hands clenching on the arms of his chair. He swallowed, his throat working as he fought to control his anger, when he did speak, his voice sounded ragged as if he would much rather have kept silent.

"A man can learn a lot out in space, Harmond. A lot of things never taught in any school, and he can meet some peculiar people out there too."

"Like who, for instance?"

"Like Professor Cantell, or have you forgotten him?"

"Cantell!" Harmond sat upright in the too-small chair. "The inventor of the nulgrav drive? Where is he?"

"That's my secret, but I know where to find him. He hasn't been wasting his time in the past fifty years."

"As long ago as that?" Harmond slumped back in the chair his eyes misty with thought. Fifty years ago, an unknown professor of science had astounded the system with the discovery of the nulgrav drive, and with the savage abruptness of an explosion mankind had headed out towards the stars. The drive was new, and it rendered Einstein's theory of relativity as something once interesting but now obsolete, it had given men the stars—and the responsibility which went with them.

"He must be a very old man now." Dell glanced at Jeff and nodded towards Harmond.

"Why?" Harmond frowned in concentration. "Let me see, he was sixty when he announced his discovery, and that was fifty years ago, that would make him one hundred and ten. With the life expectancy what it is he should be good for another thirty years yet." He laughed. "After all I'm only sixty-five and I'll bet that you're past forty, Dell?"

"Forty-three." Dell nodded and absently felt his firm jaw. "It's funny when you come to think of it, a hundred years ago and we'd have been old men by now, but ever since the longevity serum was perfected humanity can look forward to a double life span. I'm over forty, but I look no more than twenty and even Jeff here can think of himself as just past middle-age."

"Well past," grunted the big man. He looked at the ex-pilot. "What's all this about Professor Cantell?"

"He's living on one of the asteroids, a big one. I found him by accident, and he swore me to secrecy. The old man's still working, Harmond. He's managed to increase the radius of the nulgrav field, increase it enough to encompass a planetoid, and you can guess what that means."

"Yes. If he can generate a nulgrav field large enough he could move an asteroid from its orbit, swing it nearer to the sun, he could even move whole worlds! Dell! Is this what you were getting at?"

"Partially."

"You mean that there's more?"

"Yes." Dell swung in his chair and glanced out of the window. Outside the night was brilliant with stars, they glittered across the dark heavens, glittered like a handful of jewels tossed on a piece of black velvet by some careless jeweller. The tenuous thread of the Milky Way wound like some sparkling serpent from horizon to horizon.

"The Universe," he whispered. "Thousands of suns and millions of worlds waiting for the people of Earth. Think of it, Harmond. From those far off worlds comes the trade of a dozen civilisations, the nulgrav ships crossing the void above the speed of light all laden with goods and raw materials. They land on Pluto, and from there your solar ships ferry the produce to the inhabited worlds. We need that trade, Harmond, on it depends our very lives. Humanity has grown too numerous for Earth, or even for one solar system. Man has thrown off the chains of gravitation which bound him to a single sun, now we have the Galaxy to call our own."

"You make it sound too easy." Jeff twisted in his chair and glanced at the silent figure of the big man.

"I know that I do, but still, it's the truth. There are dangers of course, many dangers. Space is one, drifting fields of free radiation is another, the rogue planetoids are the worst."

"We can do nothing about them." Harmond reached for a fresh cigar. "They come from the void between the suns: dead lumps of rock, frozen and often undetectable. They sweep on their silent orbits, and each and every single one of them is a potential danger. The nulgrav ships cannot avoid them, and if the ship enters into their field of attraction, the drive fuses and the ship is left to drift powerless and helpless, drift for an eternity in the cold waste spaces between the stars."

"It happens," agreed Jeff.

"It happens too often." Harmond jerked upright in his chair. "Far too often. The crews of the nulgrav ships know it and knowing it they live while they can. On Pluto when they land the town is wide open, filled with drunken fighting crewmen working off their fear and drowning their dread of venturing again into the unknown. They hate their job, but they do it, and I doubt if they would do anything else."

"How many ships would you say have been lost through interference by the gravitational field of the rogue planetoids since the nulgrav drive was perfected?" Dell turned to face Harmond.

"How many?" The big man shrugged. "Who knows? I can tell you this, that there are over three hundred charted planetoids, and they are usually found by direct contact. When a ship blasts from Pluto, it may take years before it is expected back, and how can anyone ever keep a record of all the ships from all the planets of an entire universe?"

"The Galactic Patrol?"

"The Galactic Patrol! Who are they? Where do they come from? All we know is that when Earth finally headed towards the stars, the Galactic Patrol was out there waiting for them. Great warships, armed and armoured as spaceships could never normally be, not even with the nulgrav drive. They are always where trouble threatens, but how they get there is something no one knows. Three times during the past twenty years trade rivalry has brought Earth and the Sirian planet Vendis to the verge of interstellar war. We didn't want to fight, there was no need to fight, there are worlds enough for both civilisations to develop in peace, but they forced an ultimatum upon us, and we had no choice. Then what happened?"

"A ship of the Galactic Patrol appeared one hundred thousand miles from Earth, and another the same distance from

Vendis. We were given an ultimatum, seek peace or be blasted from space. We didn't mind, we had always wanted that, but the Vendians had to climb down." Dell paused, his brows narrowed in thought.

"I remember that! The ship was impossibly huge, and the warning came simultaneously from every radio and television screen on Earth and the system. The first race to start war would be annihilated, and somehow everyone knew that they meant just what they said. When the crisis had passed, the starship vanished, just like that! One moment it was there, the next it had gone, and nobody knows where it went."

"Does that matter now?" The old ex-pilot shifted in his chair and glared at Dell. "Let's get down to business."

"Yes." Harmond glanced at his wrist and frowned at the time. "What is your proposition?"

"This. Jeff, Cantell, you and I. Four of us, four shareholders in a new company. Cantell has the science and the new discoveries. You have a shipping line and shipbuilding yard. Jeff can introduce us to the professor and use his influence over the old man."

"Where do you come in?"

"I?" Dell smiled. "I have money, and I'm willing to use every bit of it. In case you don't think that's enough, remember this. I'm the one who can bring the parties together."

"Sounds fair enough." Harmond nodded his head. "If we do found a new company, what shall we call it, and what will it do?"

"We shall call it—" Dell frowned for a moment. "How about Planetoid Disposals Ltd., and our work will be obvious. We move planetoids, we mine the asteroids, and we destroy the rogues. Each shipping line and ship owner will pay us a retaining fee for operating expenses and servicing. We can sweep the space lanes clear of debris and assure that the nulgrav ships have an easy passage." He stared at the big man. "What can we lose? With the new ships we can operate as traders, but I know that won't be necessary."

"Right!" Harmond levered himself from the chair. "We fix details tomorrow, and I'll get to work on a franchise. We should get it almost at once."

It took five years.

CHAPTER TWO

Harmond called over the telescreen, his broad feature creased with triumph and his eyes glittering with excitement. "Dell! They've granted the franchise! After all this time, Dell! At last we can get moving!"

"Good!" Dell stared at the flushed features of his partner. "I'd just about given up hope, five years of waiting, of pouring money into the new ships and still not getting nearer to our aim. What persuaded them?"

"The latest news." Harmond wiped sweat from his face and neck. "The Vendians have beaten us to it, Dell. They have founded the Interstellar Salvage Inc., a company with much the same object as ours, but with emphasis on salvage rather than avoidance of damage. The World Federation saw the danger, we've had trouble with the Vendians before, and if they had a monopoly we'd be at their mercy."

"I see." Dell frowned in thought. "Anyway, they have granted us the franchise, does it give us full power and discretion over all planetoids?"

"Yes, there was trouble about that as we expected there would be. McKeefe, the Martian delegate wanted to know what determined a planetoid; he had the idea that we could start moving the planets if we wanted to. I talked him into seeing reason and won him over to our side. I think that when I told him that the asteroids would be the obvious ferry-point for the nulgrav ships instead of Pluto as now, he realised that Mars would benefit from the decreased freight charges."

"Naturally." Dell paused and glanced at his wrist. "Are you coming over to the shipyard? I want to let Cantell and Jeff hear the news, I know that personally I'm dying to test the new vessel."

"Yes, I'll meet you there in fifteen minutes, I want to let my wife know that I'll be late from the Council."

The screen swirled into darkness, and Dell shrugged. It seemed strange to him that the big man should be so concerned over his wife, strange that is after they had been married for so long. He smiled a little as he remembered his own marriage three years ago, but three years was a lot different from eight, in that time a mutual trust and tolerance should have replaced the natural anxiety each felt for the other.

Perhaps it was because the Harmonds were expecting their first child, and thinking of that, Dell called a number on the telescreen. A woman's fresh young features swirled into vibrant life.

"Madge?"

"Why, Dell! I didn't expect you to call so early, is anything wrong?"

"No dear, just that I wanted to see you. Are you alright?"

"Of course, dear, what a question."

"Are you sure though, Madge? You know what I mean."

"Yes, you silly old worrier, I know what you mean, but Dell try and remember that it is quite a normal thing for a woman to have a baby, even if she is over forty years old."

"You're not forty, Madge. At least you've lived that long, but you know how it is with the longevity serum, we live twice as long and age half as fast; relatively you're only twenty, and a very beautiful twenty at that."

"Fool!" She wrinkled her nose at him, far from being displeased by his obvious concern. "I'll expect you when I see you then, Dell. Have you heard from Susan?"

"No. Harmond called me and said that he'd meet me at the shipyard, he seemed a little worried about his wife."

"He shouldn't be, even though Susan insisted on having a girl, are you glad that we decided on a boy, Dell?"

"You know I am; after all, who else would I leave the company to when I'm gone?" He tried to make it sound like a joke but was sorry for the words when he saw the expression on his wife's young features.

"Dell!"

"Sorry, Madge, but please don't worry. I'll be home later. Goodbye now."

"Goodbye."

He sat and watched the screen swirl into electronic darkness.

The ship was huge, a tremendous sphere of adamantine metal housing the great nulgrav engines, the thick hull studded with the flaring orifices of the atom-rocket tubes. Cantell turned from where he sat brooding over an intricate wiring diagram and stared up at Dell's tall figure.

"I hear that the World Federation has at last granted the franchise, Dell. How soon do we start work?"

"Soon now," smiled Dell. He stared down at the withered old professor, marvelling for the hundredth time how such wonderful discoveries could flood from the brain housed in the old man's hairless skull. Cantell grinned up at him and slowly slid from the high chair. He stared at the mighty bulk of the new vessel and gestured with one claw-like hand.

"There she is, Dell, the ship I've dreamed of building ever since I discovered the nulgrav principle. One more discovery and then I can die in peace."

"Die?" Dell smiled as he looked at the wrinkled old man. "You can't die, Cantell, we need you too much, the universe needs you too much. Anyway, what is this other discovery?"

"The secret of the Galactic Patrol."

"Is that all? If you wait until you've discovered that secret, then you'll live for ever."

"No. I'm not interested in copying their secret, all I want to know is how to achieve instantaneous transmission."

"Do they have that? Couldn't it be that they can operate at tremendous high speed so that they move so fast that we just can't see them coming?"

"No, you should know better than that, Dell. Their ships appear instantaneously, and their ships are at rest, at rest, Dell! You must know what that means, and it cannot be accounted for by mere high speed."

"Very well then, Cantell, you work on the problem, and I hope that if you intend to live until you've discovered it, then you'll never die." He grinned with warm affection at the old scientist, then looked up as Harmond entered the hangar.

"Where's Jeff?"

"I saw him in town," grunted the big man, "he was trying to drink the place dry celebrating his coming good fortune, but never mind him." He looked at Cantell. "Is the ship all ready?"

"Yes."

"Good." The big man glanced at Dell. "When can we start, Dell?"

"We?"

"Naturally, I want to come too."

"No, Harmond, you can't come." Dell smiled at the expression on the big man's heavy features. "I know that you want to come on the initial flight but believe me, you just can't."

"Why not, Dell?"

"How much do you weigh, Harmond?"

"Weigh? What has that got to do with it?"

"Everything. You know the limitation governing speed on the nulgrav ships, and you know that we must travel as fast as possible. I want you to stay alive, Harmond, and one thing is certain, if you come on this new ship, you'll never see Earth again."

"I don't see it, why not?"

"You own a shipping line, and you ask me that?" Dell grinned at Cantell, the two seeming to share some private joke. "Will you tell him, professor?"

"Should I?" The little old man chuckled and winked at Dell. "Why not take him with you, work up a high speed, and then watch his blubber melt?"

"No, we can't do that, not even just to joke about it, we need him here to run the company. Tell him."

"What drives that ship, Harmond?" Cantell pointed at the smooth bulk of the new vessel.

"The nulgrav drive of course, that and atom-rocket power when near any form of mass."

"Exactly." The old man sighed and absently ran his fingers through his missing hair. "That's just the trouble, everyone mis-names the drive, they call it the nulgrav drive, and then begin to think of anti-gravity screens. It's nothing of the sort."

"Isn't it?"

"No!" Cantell felt for his stool and deliberately sat down. "I never called it that, popular indifference to the real title and ease of designation made the nulgrav drive to become known the galaxy over. The real title was 'Inhibition of inertia poten-tial within the inter-atomic particles', but whoever calls it that now?"

"No-one and I don't blame them, but how does that affect my travelling on the ship?"

"You know what happens when the field is generated? You know that Einstein's mass-velocity ratio has been disproved by my discovery? You know all that?"

"Yes."

"Very well then. Remember that the whole concept is based on the fact that to achieve speeds higher than light, the mass-ve-locity ratio had to be broken. As speed approaches that of light, so mass increases to infinity, that is the mass-velocity ratio, and it made interstellar travel an impossibility before men had even managed to reach the Moon. If mass increases to infinity, then the power needed to move that mass must also be infinite, an obvious impossibility, and so the nulgrav had to be invented before the starships could be built."

"Well?"

"The nulgrav field is generated when the ship is far from the interference of any mass, the normal distance from Earth is five hundred thousand miles, at that distance the gravitational field is weak enough to be cancelled out. The field is generated, and the main rocket drive is turned on. Now remember this, as the speed of the ship increases, the mass of the ship will increase also, at least it would if the nulgrav field were absent; when the field is used, the reverse is the case."

"I don't doubt that all this is very interesting," Harmond said dryly, "but what has it to do with my going on the ship?"

"With the field," continued the old professor calmly, "the mass of the vessel actually decreases in direct ratio to the velocity; that means that the rockets get more and more powerful the faster we go. Theoretically, the nulgrav ships have no limitation to speed, they could build up a velocity restricted only by the fuel they carry, a velocity of several hundred light years a second, except for one thing."

"Is this the important part?"

"Yes. Listen, Harmond, it may save your life." Dell gestured towards the old man. "Carry on, Cantell, you're doing a good job."

"The human body has internal pressures which cannot be ignored; blood pressure is the one we're concerned with at the moment. At high speeds the nulgrav field actually decreases the mass but it cannot decrease the internal pressure. The result is simple logic. If the restraining power of the walls of arteries and veins, of cells and capillaries is lessened without an equal lessening of the internal pressure, then the arteries and veins will burst. What actually does happen is that the capillaries go first, and the results are not very pleasant."

"You see, Harmond, you're not too good a physical specimen for high speed nulgrav flight. Your blood pressure is far too high, you would bleed through the cells and pores of the skin, the delicate capillaries feeding your brain would burst, you'd get punch-drunk, or have a stroke. You would die, Harmond, unless the speed of the ship was lessened, and in our business, we must have speed."

"I see." Harmond stood quietly for a moment, deep in thought. "Then I shall never be able to pilot one of the new ships?"

"Not at high speed, you won't, nor will you ever be able to travel on anything but the internal system rocket ships, or the passenger vessels. You know how the traders operate, the faster they can go the better. The sooner they can transmit cargos the greater their profits; no wonder they live hard while they can. The crews of the nulgrav freight ships are the toughest men in the universe, unless they were, they could never live at the high speeds they use."

"I know that, and always they have the fear that at any moment one of the rogue planetoids may approach too closely and heterodyne their nulgrav screen, leaving them drifting helplessly in outer space." Harmond shuddered at the thought. "That is what happens isn't it?"

"Mostly." Cantell frowned down at his diagram. "If the gravitational field of a planetoid heterodynes the nulgrav screen, mass returns. Sometimes it is transformed into sheer energy via the generator; in those cases, the crews are lucky, they at least remain alive, but the ship is useless except for rocket power, and inevitably they starve. At other times, if their speed is too high, or if the generator cannot handle the backlash of energy, then the ship simply explodes into atoms." He bit at his lip as he stared at the diagram, lost in a world of mental speculation.

Dell grinned down at him and gestured to the big man. Together they walked from the hangar and out into the metallic noises of the busy shipyard.

"Cantell has a problem all of his own, but it doesn't matter, he's done his part, now it's up to us." Dell watched a giant crane swing a curved hull-plate into position and narrowed his eyes at the shower of brilliant sparks from the portable welders.

"The sooner we start the better," agreed Harmond. "Our credit is running out, we must show some sort of progress or those new ships will never be built."

"We can start at once. Jeff has signed on a crew, a bunch of tough hard-bitten ex-cargo men who are accustomed to ultra speeds. My suggestion is that we go out to the asteroids and commence mining operations; at least that will give us some saleable minerals."

"No." Harmond shook his head. "That must wait. We got the franchise because of the fear of the Vendians' rival company; it would be like them to deliberately wreck ships in order to claim salvage. The World Federation thinks that they have seeded the space lanes between the suns with rogue planetoids. Our first job will be to ensure that there is a clear passage between Sol and Alpha Centauri. The distance is small, four light years, but most of our trade comes from that system, and it is important that we keep the Vendians out of our sector."

"I see. That means that we must precede the nulgrav ships, scan space for debris, and either burn the rogues with controlled atomic disintegration or affix radio-warning beacons." He halted, staring at the big man. "Wait a moment, Harmond! Who is going to pay for all this?"

"The World Federation has agreed to charter us for space sweeping and the clearance of the space lanes. We can operate under our franchise as we wish, but that was the only proviso they insisted on. I had to agree."

"Naturally, but that means we must hold ourselves at the service of the World Federation at all times." Dell frowned, his young face taut and thoughtful. "It almost makes us a space navy, a potential war-fleet, now I begin to understand more of what this is all about. The Galactic Patrol has prevented the Vendians openly declaring war, so they have founded a company which will operate a cold war. Our ships will be sabotaged, rogue planetoids deliberately sent into the paths of the nulgrav ships, vessels will be destroyed or rendered helpless—and all the time the Interstellar Salvage Inc. will be hovering around ready to pounce and claim full salvage."

"Yes, now you begin to understand how it was that we were granted an open franchise."

"I see. Planetoid Disposals Ltd. will be the answer of the World Federation, as the Vendians try to wreck our ships, so will we prevent them. It will be a battle between two rival companies—a hard relentless battle with all of space as the prize. Once the Vendians can gain control of the space lanes, they will have a strangle hold on commercial trade. Earth will become a dependent system, begging for the very necessities of existence. Vendis will have conquered Earth, and we are the only ones who can stop it."

He glanced back at the towering shape of the great hangar. "We'll leave at dawn tomorrow."

Harmond glanced at him with undisguised envy.

CHAPTER THREE

It was cold and wet, and the pale new light of dawn limned the east with a soft glow. Dell shivered, stamping his feet, and watched impatiently as the tractors dragged the vessel from the hangar. Harmond, wrapped in a thick coat and looking even larger than he was, stood beside him. Jeff lurched past, his shrewd eyes dull with the stabbing agony of a violent hangover, but determined to see the take-off.

"Nervous, Dell?"

"A little," admitted the young man. He stared at the big figure by his side. "Harmond!"

"Yes?"

"Listen, Harmond, if anything should happen to me, if for some reason I shouldn't return, look after Madge will you."

"What kind of talk is this, Dell? You'll come back and when you do, the new fleet will be ready for you to take command." Harmond grinned reassuringly. "Madge will have something for you by then also, a boy, isn't it?"

"Yes we wanted a boy." Dell grinned at the big man. "How is it that you've decided to have a girl?"

"Susan wanted one, you know that we've been hoping for a child for a long time, and when she learned that she was going to have one, she decided that it must be a girl."

"What do you think about it?"

"I like little girls, perhaps your son and my daughter will marry and found a dynasty; I think that I should like that."

"A lot can happen between now and then, and perhaps the doctors are mistaken. Perhaps they can't always determine sex before birth and arrange that the child will be either boy or girl. Maybe your son and mine will share the company, or perhaps our two daughters will go to school together."

"Not a chance!" Harmond gripped Dell's arm. "Don't worry about a single thing, Dell. I'll take care of everything at this end, don't worry about Madge. Susan will be with her, and we'll all come and meet you when you land." He glanced at the glistening vessel resting on its cradle in the open. "Better get aboard now, the tugs are waiting."

"Goodbye Harmond. Give my farewells to Cantell and see that Jeff doesn't drink us all into poverty. Goodbye."

Abruptly Dell strode towards the great spherical spaceship looming huge against the small powerful tugs. His crew was already aboard and positioned for take-off, and for a moment he felt as if he would rather do anything than climb the ramp and join them. The feeling passed, and the smooth metal of the hull reared above him.

He paused at the foot of the loading ramp, turned, and lifted an arm in farewell to the bulky figure of Harmond. The big man waved back, then the metal platform of the ramp swung on its hinges cutting off the outside view. Dell shrugged impatiently and became coldly efficient.

Lightly he ran up the short flights of stairs to the control room and strapped himself into the cushioned pilot's chair. Rapidly he scanned the banked instruments before him and brushed his hand over a row of instruments. "Control room to crew. Stand by for take-off." He closed fresh circuits. "P.D.L. Vessel one calling booster tugs. Are you with me?"

"Booster tugs with you. PDL I."

"Take-off immediate. Warning five. Blast together on zero." Dell activated his main rocket drive, and beneath the base of the vessel a giant began to mutter as the gaping orifices of the atom-rocket tubes spouted flame. Tensely he sat, his fingers hovering delicately on the firing control as he watched the swinging hand of a chronometer.

"Ready! Five! Four! Three! Two! One! Fire!" Almost savagely he pressed down the firing control.

Flame gushed from the idling rockets. Flame superheated and searing the thick concrete of the shipyard, fusing the stubborn material and causing it to flow like mud. The great ship trembled, shuddering beneath the thrust of the spouting tubes, lifting a little, slowly and almost painfully towards the heavens.

Beside them the booster tugs sent snarling echoes thundering through the still morning air as they strained at the attached cables. Without them, the great new vessel could never tear itself away from the gravitational field of the planet; once free of the grip of a world, it would never return. None of the nulgrav ships ever did, they were too big, too underpowered without the nulgrav screen to assist their rockets ever to land on any large world. They swung in orbits while ferry boats shifted their cargos.

Tensely Dell watched his instruments as the thunder from the streaming rockets mounted into a whistling scream. He glanced at the three booster tugs, each a tiny cabin above fuel tanks and mammoth rocket engines and narrowed his eyes against the fierce blue-white glare of their rocket blast. Beneath him, the Earth began to fall away.

The shipyard became a dot, then was lost in a maze of green and brown. Rivers became mere threads, and the sullen grey of a distant sea smeared the horizon, then clouds swirled about the view plates, and the sun blazed in all its unshielded glory. Higher they climbed, higher, the air whistling past their hull with a thin scream raising the temperature a few degrees with the friction of its passing. The blue the sky deepened, grew black, the blackness of space spangled with the glittering points of countless stars.

Abruptly the radio crackled into life. "Booster tugs to PDL 1. Casting off."

"PDL I to boosters. Thanks."

The magnetic fastenings of the cables jerked open, and Dell felt the surge of power as he operated the firing controls. The tugs fell away behind him, and with all main tubes spouting flame he headed for outer space.

Six hundred thousand miles from Earth he engaged the nulgrav drive.

A thin whine raced through the hull, quivering through the metal of deck-plates and bulkheads. It echoed with a faint metallic chiming from the transparent plastic of the observation ports and the instrument covers, it hung tinkling on the air within the ship, it seemed to penetrate the very bone and muscle of the tensely waiting crew.

A ripple surged from the nulgrav engines, a sub-atomic movement more sensed than seen, a subtle adjustment of the electro-wave fluid between the very components of the atoms themselves. It pulsed, wavered a little, then aside from a thin thread of humming sound, the ship was as before.

Delicately Dell increased the engine power. Behind them long streamers of blue-white flame stabbed into space as the swift moving ions from the rocket engines sped through their exhausts and thrust against the great hull. The ship began to move faster, faster, even faster. As the humming nulgrav field reduced the actual mass of the vessel in inverse ratio to their speed, the acceleration began to mount in disproportionate ratio. Ahead of them glittered the target-star of Alpha Centauri.

Dell sighed and grinned at the astrogator sitting in his duel seat. "Nice easy take-off; I'd half expected to be crushed back in the chair."

"Why?" The astrogator stretched and smiled in memory of the old days. "That used to be the thing, when you had to reach escape velocity in as short a time as possible. Now we use the booster tugs and rise just as comfortably as if we used an elevator." He stared at the visi-screen. "What speed do you intend reaching?"

"The maximum. I want to take an outward sweep to Alpha, then sweep back. Keep your eye on the radar at all times."

"Will it be of any use?" The astrogator looked at the compact instrument housing. "I've been on ships with radar detectors before, they work fine—if you've the time to read their signals, but we're travelling faster than light, or we soon will be, and the signal will be gone before we know it."

"This is a special kind of radar." Dell grinned at the man's expression. "In a way it isn't radar at all, though we call it that, it is really a mass detector, and we can spot anything of a mass one hundred thousandth part of that of our own, in other words, anything a hundred times too small to hurt us."

"Then what do we do?"

"Stop the ship, track and destroy it, remove it from the shipping lanes for ever."

"I see." The astrogator stared at the blank screen of the instrument. "I've been on many a nulgrav cargo ship, and some of them even carried a few instruments, but none of them ever carried anything like this."

"Why should they?" Dell tried not to sound bitter. "That scanning device weighs several tons and costs quite a lot of money. The only instrument most freight ships carry is one that doesn't weigh a gram and costs nothing at all."

"Yes?" The astrogator looked interested. "Which one is that?"

"Blind luck!"

"What?"

"Luck, blind luck. What does the average nulgrav captain do? He aims his ship at a target-star, throws in his screen and fires his main drive. He accelerates until the blood begins seeping from his skin, then he cuts gravs. After while he releases his screen and blasts into port."

"Off port," corrected the astrogator, "the ferry boats do the rest."

"I know that, but what does the freight ship captain do to protect his crew?"

"Nothing, though I believe that some of them pray a little." The astrogator seemed very thoughtful. "After all what can they do?"

"Nothing, except as you said, pray. That's why we're here. We're going to remove every obstacle threatening the space lanes, and we're starting with the Sol-Alpha Centauri route."

A green speck flashed on the screen, and a red lamp flickered warningly. The astrogator leaned tensely over his instruments while Dell studied his controls.

"Got it?"

"Yes. Mass approx. twenty tons, flight pattern within one tenth parsec of regular space lane. Uncharted, metallic content of fifty percent, surface temperature, zero."

"Our first job!" Dell pressed on the panel before him, and an alarm shrilled deep within the ship. "Attention! Attention! Party number one prepare for outside action! Leave at once, co-ordinates are—" Dell rattled off a stream of figures, and with a brief spurt of flame from its stubby driving tubes, the auxiliary vessel left the parent ship.

"What are they going to do?"

"Set up a controlled atomic disintegration radio beam," Dell supplied. "At faster-than-light speed the flame of the atomic fire will not be seen, but it will register in the brain, and I had a friend once who went insane after a single trip. He shipped as engine room attendant on a tramp freighter and the skipper pushed the ship as fast as he could stand. Two of the crew died before he would cut gravs and my friend never signed on again." The astrogator stared dully at the blank screen of the mass detector.

"I looked for that skipper for a long time, but I never found him. He vanished on the very next trip, probably he's drifting somewhere between the suns a thing of bone and tattered cloth in an empty hull."

Abruptly the detector sparkled with green, and the warning lamp filled the cabin with a lurid glare. Dell spun to his controls, and the astrogator stooped over his instruments.

"I can't track it, Dell! It's moving, a ship I swear that it's a ship!"

"Ships don't move except on a straight line," snapped Dell impatiently. "Plot their flight path and we'll blast to avoid!"

"I can't!" The astrogator stared at Dell, his eyes sick and mad looking. "It's manoeuvring straight towards us!"

"Impossible!" Dell spun the astrogator away from the screen and stared with hard eyes at the drifting green speck. "You're right!" he snapped. "That is a ship, the skipper must he insane!"

He pressed alarm buttons on the instrument panel.

"Control to ship. Strap down. Prepare for course-change!"

Tensely he sat with his hands hovering over the controls, waiting for the split second when he must blast the ship away from the strange vessel. He stiffened at a cry from the astrogator and glanced quickly at the detector screen. It was alive with little green flecks, all space seemed to be filled with objects and they all seemed to be heading straight towards the ship.

Desperately he blasted the ship out of their line of flight. The rockets spouted great tongues of blue-white fire as they strained to veer the huge vessel, and for one brief moment he thought that they had won clear, then a groan from the astrogator jerked his eyes to the detector screen. Fresh flecks of green light filled the blankness!

"They fired at us!" The astrogator swore dully as he watched the approaching missiles. "That ship, I watched it as it veered away. It fired something at us, and we can't get away!"

"We can try!" Dell spun back to his firing controls. Blood rushed from his head at the terrible thrust of acceleration, and something warm and salty to the taste trickled from his eyes and nose. The ship creaked, the hull plates twisting beneath the savage thrust of the great driving tubes, and on the detector screen the little menacing flecks of green dropped away.

For a moment Dell felt a rush of triumph as he saw the cleared screen, then— The nulgrav engines screamed beneath the lash of terrible forces. Something smashed against the hull and the gravitational field of the unknown object heterodyned the delicate nulgrav field within the ship itself.

Space strained as the throbbing power of the mighty engines fought to hold the screen in stasis, fought, and failed as the intermeshed fields swung the balance of power into normal lines.

The ship trembled, twisted, shuddered as full mass returned with the disruption of the field. Mass flooded back into the vessel, titanic mass, mass impossible to contain, it transformed into sheer energy, blasted through the nulgrav generator, and poured from there into outer space. For seconds the ship was a writhing conflict of streaming energies, then silence and the pale flickering of the emergency fights.

Dell shuddered and lifted himself painfully from the cushioned pilot's chair. He glanced at the astrogator and could tell by the man's twisted features that he was dead. Painfully he crawled through the ship.

The nulgrav generator was a mass of fused and useless metal. Staring at it, Dell felt an inward sickness at the knowledge of inevitable death.

CHAPTER FOUR

Framed against the star-shot night of space the planetoid was a jagged mass of frozen rock twenty miles in diameter. It slowly rotated, the imbedded minerals on its crust reflecting the starlight in little glimmers of red and blue and orange. One side seemed to have been sheered away by some cosmic force the rest of the little world thrust needle spires towards the glittering stars.

Men moved over the jagged surface, spacesuited men working with great machines and among them metallic shine. A spaceship gleamed, a thing of peerless beauty, poised a few miles from the planetoid.

Steve Franson stood in the control cabin and stared with interest at the scene reflected in the visi-screen. He was tall and seemed to have a brittle hardness, his eyes were cold and at times almost cruel. He wore rough spaceman's leather, and a thin scar traced a path down one cheek.

"Tell them to speed it up," he snapped at a man standing beside him. "The nulgrav generators should have been fixed by now, and the planetoid ready to move."

"Yes, sir. Will you superintend the operation?"

"No. I'm wanted back at Canton. You can manage it; you know the new orbit. Get the opencast mining started as soon as the sun has melted the surface ice."

"I'll do that." The mining engineer stared at the young man. "How will you get to Canton, sir? Shall I radio for a rocketship, or will you pilot an auxiliary?"

"Neither. Harmond said that he'd send for me." He glanced at the visi-screen. "That looks like my ship now, get those men moving…we need that metal."

He swung from the control cabin, and donning a spacesuit, entered the airlock. No sooner had the newly arrived ship made contact, he swung himself across the few yards of open space and entered the vessel. A girl grinned at him from the pilot's chair.

"Steve! That was quick."

"Hello, Madge. I thought that you were in a hurry."

"I am."

"Well?"

"Sorry." She reddened a little and turned to the controls. Almost savagely she operated the firing controls and with a jerk the rocket ship blasted away from the poised spaceship. Steve grunted beneath the acceleration pressure and grimly fought his way into the dual pilot's seat.

"I didn't say we were in that much of a hurry."

"We should be." Madge adjusted the controls and turned to the young man. "Cantell is dying, Steve, it's a miracle that he's managed to live for so long, but this time the doctors have no hope."

"Cantell dying?" Steve bit his lips and suddenly seemed very young and boyish. "I shall miss the old man; he was one of the last. Jeff dead in a drunken brawl on Vendis, my father dead while testing the very first ship, both your mother and mine dead when a nulgrav ship hit a planetoid." He sighed. "That leaves your father, Madge, he is the last of the original company."

"I know, and it won't be long before he is dead too, Steve."

"What?"

"You know what happened to him when he tried to find your father. He drove the ship too fast and suffered for it. He lay partially paralysed for ten years and the doctors say that if he ever tries to travel on a nulgrav ship again, it will kill him."

"Then he mustn't travel!"

"He will, Steve. This war with Vendis has him all worked up, for thirty years we have been fighting on their terms and we're losing. Steve, you know that."

"I don't think that we are losing."

"Perhaps you don't, but then you don't remember the old days of free trade. My father does, and he is worried about what has happened since then."

"The Galactic Patrol will stop any war, Madge. There's need for us to worry about it."

"There is, Steve, there's plenty to worry about."

"Maybe there is, then, but worrying won't do any good." She glanced at him, shrugged, and turned again to the controls. For a while they travelled in silence, the faint vibration of the rockets quivering through the hull. Before them the sun expanded into a great yellow ball, and once they passed a nulgrav ship heading at high speed towards theirs.

Steve glanced after it, a look of envy in his cold grey eyes.

"Like to be on her, Steve?"

"Why not? I'm sick of swinging planetoids across the system. I want to be out there where the stars are glittering points and no sun is recognisable."

"Why don't you? Your ships travel the space lanes clearing the star paths. You could go with one whenever you choose."

"Could I?" Steve smiled without humour. "Ask your father about that, Madge. He is the one who is keeping me bound to the solar system. I know that one day I shall head the company, but at the moment your father is in full charge."

"You envy him don't you, Steve?"

"No, Madge. I admire your father, and I've done everything he told me to do ever since I was old enough to remember, but I'm tired of study, Madge. I want to enjoy what our fathers dreamed of, and what my father died for."

"The Universe?"

"Yes."

She fell silent staring at the expanding ball of the sun, and after a while Steve gently shook her by the shoulder.

"Wake up, Madge, Canton lies dead ahead."

"Want to take her in?"

"No, you're as good a pilot as I am, you make the landing."

Harmond met them on the landing field. He had grown very old, and his huge figure seemed shrunken and withered a little as if all life had been drained away. He smiled at Steve and kissed his daughter, then led the way across the tiny field towards a group of buildings.

"Madge tells me that the old man is dying, is that true?"

"Yes, Steve. Cantell is going fast. It's not surprising really, after all he's a hundred and forty years old now, and even with the longevity serum, no man can expect to live forever."

"I am glad that you sent for me, I want to see him again before he dies."

"You shall, Steve, he is waiting for you."

Together they entered the building. Cantell lay on inflated mattress, a withered little husk of a man, his hairless scalp gleaming in the soft light of the hidden fluorescents. Racks of medicines rested against one wall and several electronic physiotherapy machines stood near at hand. Steve was surprised to see a large drawing board swung on a stand near the bed, and the white sheets were covered with scraps of paper dark with scribbled equations.

A man in a white smock hovered near at hand and nodded at Harmond's questioning glance. "He is resting quietly now, sir, but he is very weak. I doubt that he will live another twenty-four hours."

"I see...will our visit harm him?"

"No, it may do him good." The doctor sounded as nothing now had the power to harm the old man very much. When a man's life can be measured in hours, he is beyond harm.

Gently Steve looked down at the old man and was surprised to see that Cantell was smiling at him, with a merry glitter in his old weak eyes.

"Hello, son."

"Hello, Prof." He forced himself to smile. "They tell me t you're laying down on the job, don't you remember what you once told my father?"

"I remember," the old man's voice sounded like the faint buzzing of some tiny insect.

"Well? What are you wasting your time in here for?"

Cantell chuckled, and his thin old claw-like hand grasped Steve's big fist in affection. "Always joking aren't you, son? Just like your father, he was always teasing me too." A shadow darkened the thin old features. "A good man your father, Steve. I wonder if I shall meet him again—out there?"

"Maybe, Prof, anything is possible."

"Is Harmond here?"

"Yes." The big man stepped up beside Steve and smiled down at the wasted figure on the bed.

"Good. I must talk to you, talk to you both." Fire burned briefly in the faded eyes. "I've done it, Steve! I've done what I said I would, and now I can die in peace."

"What!" Steve glanced at the impassive face of Harmond, then stared at the old man. "You're joking!"

"No. No I'm not joking, I've solved the final secret, the secret of the Galactic Patrol. Instantaneous transmission!"

"Impossible!" Harmond glanced at Steve and frowned warningly. "What is it, Cantell?"

"You always said that it was impossible, Harmond, but then so did a thousand other fools when I discovered nulgrav, and is that impossible? I tell you I've solved the equations governing instantaneous transmission, I've solved it I tell you. I've solved it!"

The doctor stepped forward and frowned at the big man. He sprayed some chemical beneath the old man's nose and gently pressed him back onto his pillow.

"Please be careful not to excite him," he said sharply. "I cannot be responsible for what may happen if you ignore this warning."

"Get that fool out of here," snapped Cantell. "I've lived too long to be beaten at the last, and I've got to convince you that I know what I'm talking about."

"Alright, Prof," soothed Steve. "I believe you; you know that."

"Yes, Steve, yes. I've trained you, and now you know as much about nulgrav as I do. But Harmond took you from me too soon."

"I had to teach the boy the tricks of space," rumbled Harmond. "It was no use him knowing the theory without learning the practice."

"Never mind that now," snapped the old man impatiently. "Look, Steve, I've written all the equations down and partly designed some of the machinery. I'll swear that it will work, but I can't do it myself, Steve, I can't do it myself. You must take over now, you and Harmond. Promise me that you'll do it, Steve. Promise!"

"Yes, Prof, of course we promise. Lie down now and get some rest."

"Rest! What do I want with rest? Anyone would think that I'm an old man, but I'm not, I'm only really half the age I've lived, and a man used not to be old at seventy. Why should I be old now?"

"Lie down," insisted Steve. "You've done more in your lifetime than any other five men, naturally you've worn yourself out, but don't be greedy. Give us younger men a chance."

Cantell grinned, his thin lips writhing in a ghastly attempt at humour, but he rested back on his inflated pillow.

"You're right as usual, Steve." He stared at the ceiling. "It is based on electrons you know, on the fact that each and every electron is identical with every other electron. There is no difference, Steve, no difference at all. Do you understand?"

"I think that I do." The young man frowned in thought, and then shrugged as Harmond tugged at his sleeve. "Tell me about it."

"Don't tire him," whispered Harmond.

"Tire him?" Steve smiled and bit his lips as he stared own at the pitiful wasted figure on the bed. "Can't you understand, Harmond? He's dying, he knows it, and there's nothing anyone can do about it. Talking about his discovery will take his mind off thinking about the end. Tire him? I'm doing him the very best favour one man could do to another."

"Everything is made of electrons, Steve, everything. There are other parts to an atom, that we know, but the electron is truly universal. Instantaneous transmission, Steve, the crossing of space without the loss of a single instant of time. We can do it, Steve, we can do it…we can do—"

The thin little voice died away, and for a moment Steve stared down at the silent figure of the old man, knowing what had happened, but refusing for a moment to accept that knowledge.

"Cantell!" The doctor moved on silent feet closer to the bed. "Professor, answer me!" Carefully the man in the white smock lifted the thin arm and felt the scrawny wrist.

"Prof, talk to me; it's Steve here. Prof!"

Gently the doctor covered the staring features of the thin old man, and with that gesture Steve knew that Professor Cantell had entered another state.

He stumbled a little as he left the building, feeling the cold sickness of emotion trapped within him, held by the iron chains of rigid convention. He had never known his father, and his mother had died in a futile attempt to find the lost vessel, within the second year of his life. Cantell had been both father and mother to him, for Harmond had driven himself like a dog to found the company, and now Cantell was dead.

He was grateful that the others left him alone.

CHAPTER FIVE

Canton was an artificial world, a planetoid captured in deep space and swung into an orbit mid-way between Ear and Mars. An adaption of the nulgrav field had given it an earth type gravity, and with its blue sky and warm soft air it was a haven for the hard-bitten crews of the nulgrav ships.

Harmond stood at the edge of the small private landing field and stared at the near horizon, his heavy features sagged a little and he seemed to be very tired.

"Steve, I want to talk with you. Madge, will you take the ship and meet us later?"

"Yes, father, at the main building?"

"Yes. Ready, Steve?"

"Must we—now?"

"I think so. I know how you must be feeling about Cantell's death, but things are urgent Steve. We must have a conference."

"As you wish." Dully Steve followed the big man into a waiting ground car, and rapidly they swept across the little world towards the great main space port.

Soaring high into the soft air, the building of Planetoid Disposals Ltd dominated the entire scene. Resting on the edge of the scarred landing field, the smooth plastic of its outer construction illuminated by the stabbing light from the ferry boat rocket blasts, it represented the single hope of a race driven by undeclared war to a point of desperation.

Harmond stared at the activity on the landing field, and his heavy features darkened with anger. "Look at them, Steve! Look at them." He pointed with a finger that trembled with rage.

"I see them." The young man stared coldly at the trim ships resting on the landing field. Strange vessels these, slender and with gaping orifices ringing bow and stem. Gun turrets marred their smooth hulls and the squat barrels of deadly weapons snouted menacingly towards the stars.

"Ships of the Interstellar Salvage Inc. What are they doing here?"

"That is why I must talk with you, but look at them Steve. Why should salvage vessels be armed?"

"They say in case they land on alien worlds, for defence only in case of need."

"Do you believe that?"

"It sounds reasonable," the young man said slowly, "but—?"

"Let's go up to the office." Harmond swung into the towering building, and a silent elevator whisked them to the private offices. Guards, looking respectfully at the tall figure of the young man, nominal head of the greatest space fleet and most important company in the history of man, saluted respectfully as they passed. Harmond snapped quick orders. His voice was heavy with fatigue and worry. "Seal this sector, let none enter except my daughter."

"Yes, sir."

Thick doors slid behind them and for the first time since Steve had landed on Canton, he saw Harmond relax a little. The big man slumped down into a chair and fumbled for a cigar. Impatiently he tried to still the trembling of his hands as he strove to light the thick cylinder, then smiled in weak gratitude as Steve did it for him.

"Thanks, son, and now let's get down to a few facts."

"Look, Harmond, I'm busy and I know that you can run things far better than I ever could. Must I stay here?"

"Yes." Harmond glanced at the young man in sudden doubt. "What have you to do that's so important?"

"They're bringing in a new planetoid, one of the biggest so far. I wanted to make sure that nothing went wrong."

"Leave it."

"I have," said Steve dryly, "now I'd like to get back to work."

"It isn't important now, Steve; none of that work matters now, not to you."

"No?"

"No." Harmond sighed and sent a thick coil of blue smoke drifting across the silent room. "We're at war, Steve. We've been at war for thirty years now, and we're losing that war."

"The trade war you mean, or the private war between Planetoid Disposals and Interstellar Salvage?"

"They are the same war."

"Are they?" The young man smiled and gently shook his head. "I doubt it, after all what have we to do with trade? Interstellar Salvage has tried to run us out of the Galaxy, that I know, but we operate on entirely different lines of business. We should work together, not be at each other's throats all the time."

"Are you mad, Steve? Have you gone insane?" Harmond stared at the young man and tried to control his temper. He crushed out the cigar, and his hand trembled as he released the charred stub.

"No, Harmond, I'm not insane, but I think that you've lived with a single thing for too long. Planetoid Disposals has been your life, you see everything in relation to it. Another company is a threat to universal dominance."

"I see." The big man breathed deeply for a moment and gently shook his head. "All this is partly my fault, Steve. I've kept you secluded for too long. Here within the solar system you haven't seen what I have, you haven't seen burnt and gutted ships, murdered crews, spoiled cargoes. You haven't seen how our trade has fallen, and how Earthmen have lost prestige throughout the galaxy. We are fighting a war, Steve, like it or not. It wasn't of our choosing, and we want no part of it, but we're in it, and we've got to win!"

"The Galactic Patrol will take care of any war."

"Will they? Trade war can be as harmful as any other kind of battle. You know that we depend on imports from the stars to keep our factories working, our people fed. The nulgrav ships rove the galaxy bringing in raw materials and other essential produce, and in return we export machinery, fabricated items, and goods which other races cannot make. We must trade, Steve; if we don't, then we starve!"

"That is history, Harmond, what has it to do with us?"

"We are the guardians of the space lanes, Steve. On the work of our ships the free flow of trade depends, the lifeblood of our civilisation. We are dedicated to keeping the star routes free, and we've done it for thirty years now."

"I know all that." The young man glanced out of the window to the space port far below. A ferry boat rose with a shrill scream from its spouting venturis, and for a moment the fierce glare from the rocket exhaust stained the room with brilliant colour.

"Then why argue about it, son?"

"Because it all seems so futile. We dispose of the rogue planetoids, sweeping them from the space lanes, destroying them, burning them to atomic dust. The Vendians operate a salvage company, they assist the wrecked vessels, acting as guardians for any ship unfortunate enough to founder in space. We should work together, not apart."

"Steve!"

The young man glanced at Harmond, struck by the seriousness in the older man's tones. "Yes?"

"Have you ever thought of how your father died?"

"He was operating the very first ship of the new company. It never returned."

"Exactly, but have you never stopped to think why it didn't return?"

"Accident."

"No. Not on that vessel, not built as we built it."

"Then what?"

"Intent, Steve. We launched that ship shortly after Interstellar Salvage commenced operations. Your father left to clear the Sol Alpha Centauri route, a mere four light years of distance.

He never returned, and for a long time we wondered just as you have whether or not it could have been accident or not, but now we know."

"We know! How?"

"I received this only yesterday, it was found by the commander of one of our ships on routine patrol." Harmond tossed a metal cylinder onto the polished surface of the desk. "It is a recording instrument, and it was found drifting in space attached to a radio beacon. It was by sheer chance that it was found; its mass is far too small to bother about but something about the radio frequency intrigued the commander and he stopped to pick it up. I have rewarded him for his trouble."

"Yes?"

"It is a recording of your father's voice, Steve. The last recording he made, and he knew even then that he was going to die. Do you want to hear it?"

The young man hesitated, then looked appealingly at the big figure slumped in the chair. "Should I?"

For answer Harmond slipped the metal cylinder into small machine and threw a switch. A grating came from hidden speaker, a scratching, and a faint whirring sound.

"The free radiation of space has damaged it a little," Harmond explained. "Listen."

A voice echoed dully from the speaker, a man's voice, tense and gritty with strain. It sounded against a background of creaking metal and the soft whisper of released energies; it spoke across time and space, and for a moment the room became transformed into the harsh metal and thinning air of a wrecked spaceship cabin.

"This is Franson calling, Dell Franson…will the finder of the message please deliver it to the offices of the Planetoid Disposals Ltd."

For a moment the machine hummed in discordant static, then: "Harmond? I don't know if this will ever reach you, or if it is ever found, whether you will still be alive. Not that it matters now, nothing can ever matter to me again. The ship was wrecked, by now you may know that, but it wasn't accident that wrecked us, it was deliberate destruction. We had just passed the edge, just over one light speed, when the screen registered a large quantity of mass. I tried to veer away from it, but it followed, and by that I knew that the object must be a ship. They fired on us, Harmond! They blasted space with missiles, each of them capable of heterodyning the nulgrav field. I tried to veer away but it was impossible, and the field collapsed on impact. I know that I am going to die; the generator is wrecked, and atomic fires have been started in the storeroom. I am recording this and will eject it attached to a radio beacon. Do what you can, Harmond, and one other thing—look after my son." The machine hummed softly; the recording ended.

Steve took a shuddering breath. "I never knew my father," he whispered, "was that his voice?"

"Yes."

"I see." Steve rose from his chair and crossing the room stared out of the window. "They murdered him, left him to drift between the stars." Unconsciously he clenched his lists.

"That is what I wanted to talk to you about." Harmond swung in his chair and looked towards the young man. "It is time that you took full command of the company."

"Later, I have something to do first."

"Revenge?" The big man shook his head and joined Steve at the window. For a moment they stood side by side staring down at the activity below, their faces lit by the almost constant glare of rocket blasts.

"They killed my father," whispered Steve, "would it be so wrong to kill them?"

"That is not the way."

"No? What is?"

"Beat them at their own game. If it is to be war, then let us fight on equal terms. You have read our franchise and you know on what grounds it was granted to us. We are to hold ourselves at the disposal of the World Federation. You know what that means, we are the space fleet of Earth, our ships are the warships protecting our solar system, and you are supreme commander."

"I am?"

"Yes. It is what you have been trained for all your life. Eventual command of the company and all that such command entails. Don't you realise it even now, Steve? On you depends the welfare of our civilisation. Your ships are one barrier between us and the Vendian dream of galactic conquest, once the tide begins to swing against us, then Earth as the home of a free people is doomed."

Far below on the edge of the landing field one of slender shapes of the Interstellar Salvage fleet moved a little with a flare of brilliant jets. It jerked, slithered on the thick concrete of the space port sending plumes of dust writhing from beneath its broad landing skids, then the jets died, and the dust settled on the glistening hull.

A ship, its round thick hull sparkling with signal lights thundered high above the landing field, the flame from exhausts throwing every little detail of the busy field into sharp relief. Harmond glanced up at it and smiled a little with quiet pride.

"Look, Steve! PDL 807 just fresh from the yards and there are plenty more like her almost ready to blast." He squinted his eyes against the fierce glare of the settling vessel. "Like the first ship, this one can operate under her own power within the gravity field of any planet up to five Earth gravities. The nul-grav drive can be used one hundred thousand miles from Earth, instead of five hundred thousand."

"Is she armed?" Steve shielded his eyes as he stared the descending ship. "I can see turrets."

"Naturally she is armed—for defence if ever she lands on an alien world," Harmond said dryly. "The turrets can be used for more than mere defence however. We have installed launching tubes for guided atomic rocket missiles; they are to be used to burn rogue planetoids without stopping the ship or sending out a work party."

"I see; neutronium-headed of course."

"Yes, each torpedo will have high mass, enough to make sure that once within the gravitational attraction of a planetoid it will never leave." The big man's face darkened. "Something like that must have been used to wreck your father's vessel, and I'm certain that half the lost nugrav ships are due to a neutronium bomb placed in their flight paths."

"It may be as you say, but how can we ever prove it? The Interstellar Salvage Inc. always manage to have one of their ships nearby to save the crew and cargo; they could also reclaim the bomb, and probably do."

"I have proof enough." Harmond stood and glowered down at the rival vessels; they rested, slender darts against the round bulk of the newly arrived ship the multiple guns their turrets swinging a little from time to time.

"Can't we contact the Galactic Patrol?"

"I don't know, as far as I know it has never been done, but I'm doing what I can. I'm broadcasting on both beam dispersed radio and sub-etheric impulses. If they have a listening post anywhere in the galaxy, they must be able to pick up my appeal, but that doesn't mean that they are going do anything about it."

"Why not, this situation is threatening the peace of the universe, they must interfere."

"No. We are in no actual danger of interstellar war; the trade war can cripple our civilisation, but it does not endanger our planet as a shooting war would."

Down on the distant space port the slender vessel of the rival company shifted again on flaring jets, the heavy guns the forward turrets lifting as the vessel slewed. They swung, steadied, and for a moment Steve stared directly into the snouting orifices.

"Look at that ship!" He gestured with one hand. "What does the captain think that he's doing?"

"Where?" Harmond leaned closer to the window, eyes narrowed as he stared into the flame-shot darkness the space port.

"There! You can see how they've slewed their ship ready for immediate take-off. Look at those fore-guns, if I didn't know better, I'd think that they were about to fire at us."

"Impossible!" The big man shook his head in disbelief. "They just wouldn't dare to fire their guns over a crowded space port, they just wouldn't dare!"

"Perhaps you're right." Steve watched as the menacing guns seemed to shift a little, and again he had the idea that someone hidden within the turret was taking careful deliberate aim. Abruptly something smashed into his side and thrown off balance he reeled from the window and fell heavily to the floor.

"What—?"

Fire splashed against the plastic, searing blinding energy bursting the transparent window as if it were paper and streaming into the room. Energy lashed from the walls, filling the room with heat and smoke and the electronic smell of released ozone.

Steve rolled on to the floor, covering his face with folded arms and feeling the flesh of his neck and hands crisp and sear beneath the savage blast of energy. His breath burned in his lungs and he could feel his spaceman's leather char and smoulder as the free energy lashed at him. Then it was over, and he could see again.

Something lay beneath the window, a charred heap of smouldering cloth and seared tissue. A shapeless mass of what had once been a man, huddled on the burnt flooring and unrecognisable as anything that had once been human.

"Harmond!" Steve felt sick as he looked at the huddled figure. "Harmond!"

From the space port came the thunder of rockets.

CHAPTER SIX

Guards burst into the still smoking room, weapons in their hands and their eyes hard and cold as they saw what lay beneath the smashed window. Steve glanced at them, then past them to where the slender shape of a young girl stood, one hand pressed to her mouth and her eyes wide with shocked horror.

"Madge! Don't come in here. Don't enter this room!"

"Steve! My father is he—?"

"Yes, Madge, and I'm going to get those that did it."

Impatiently he waited for the elevator, and when it came, jerked with the tension of his nerves as it dropped to the lower regions. Men stared at him as he raced from the building and across the fire-marked concrete of the landing field. The newly arrived ship loomed before him, then the slender shapes of the Vendians' ships, two now where there had been three.

A crowd milled around them, a crowd of tough hard bitten cargo hands and nulgrav traders. Others made up the crowd, the neatly uniformed personnel of Planetoid Disposals Ltd., and the angry hum of their voices lifted to the star-studded sky.

Desperately Steve forced his way through the crowd until he faced the lowered ramp of the Vendian ship. A man stood negligently at the top of the ramp, a man dressed in the black and scarlet of Vendis. He leaned against the hull of his ship, and he wore two heavy flare-guns belted to his waist.

"Where is the man who fired that shot?" Steve strode towards the loading ramp and set one foot on the smooth metal.

"An accident, I must apologise." The Vendian smiled, his blue teeth gleaming against the yellow of his lips and the blue of his skin. Unlike Earthmen, the Vendians had a copper base for their blood, and it made it blue instead of the red of iron.

"Accident?" Steve strode forward his anger like a living coal within his brain. The Vendian straightened, his eyes with their vertical pupils narrowing like those of a cat.

"Get off my ship!"

"Your ship?" Curtly Steve laughed and turned to the crowd. "His ship he says, and one of his friends has just killed Harmond." He stared at the Vendian, his eyes narrowed and hard. "I want that man, do you give him to me, or do I come in and take him?"

"He is not here, and it was an accident I tell you. A mechanic was cleaning the guns, and his finger tripped the release; it was unfortunate that the blast damaged your building, but the damage will be paid for."

"Where is the man?"

"He was on the other ship. I am here to settle any claim which you may have."

Abruptly the Vendian straightened, the squat barrel of a flare-gun steady in one hand. "Now get off my ship," he snarled. "Earth scum! Move or I'll blast you to atoms!"

"If it was an accident, then why should the man leave?" Steve looked at the Vendian and slowly shook his head. "You knew all about what was to happen, I saw you manoeuvring your ships just before the blast, you were taking aim even then, and I didn't guess what was going to happen." He took a long stride forward. "Someone is going to pay for that murder!"

"I've warned you!" The gun in the Vendian's hand swung level with Steve's stomach and the young man could see the tension of the trigger finger. "Get off that ramp or I'll fire!"

Something hurled past Steve's head, a spanner thrown by one of the watching crowd. It struck the Vendian's wrist, and the flare-gun clattered to the metal of the ramp, and simultaneously with the half-seen movement, the young man stepped forward.

His fist smashed into a blue face, and his knuckles split against the other's teeth. Spitting like a cat the Vendian staggered, then sprang forward, his hands curved like claws, and one heavy boot swinging in a vicious kick towards Steve's groin.

Desperately Steve twisted his body taking the full force of the kick against the muscles of his thigh. He staggered, his whole leg feeling numb from the blow, then almost fell beneath a rain of blows. Hands clawed at his face, the long nails seeking his eyes, and a knee thrust at him bringing a wave of sheer agony. Grimly the young man fought back, twisting his head to save his eyes and feeling the long nails of the Vendian tear at his skin.

He smashed his fists against a body which seemed made of muscle and bone, driving terrible blows deep into the other's stomach and pounding at the blue face. Tissue pulped beneath his knuckles and the Vendian screamed with the pain of a broken nose. Blood-stained Steve's fist, red blood and blue, and still he smashed at the contorted features of the alien feeling a savage satisfaction in dealing out punishment to a member of a race which had held Earth in contempt for too long.

Men pushed past the struggling couple, men screaming with released anger, the tough crews of the nulgrav ships who travelled in constant fear of death, and who blamed the Vendians for that fear. Within the ship metal smashed and suddenly the squat turret guns blasted a thunderous note of raw destruction.

Steve writhed in the Vendian's grasp, smashed a crippling blow at the other's exposed throat, then drove his hard fist against a suddenly undefended jaw. Eyes glazed, the Vendian slumped to the cold metal of his deck plates, and wiping the blood from his eyes, Steve glanced about him.

The space port was a scene of utter confusion. Men raced from the attendant buildings, and little knots of them battled furiously in a dozen subsidiary conflicts. The second of the two Interstellar Salvage Inc. vessels rested in a pool of molten metal, blasted by the fire from its sister ship's captured guns. A siren wailed from a group of low roofed buildings, and several car-loads of uniformed police began to break up the struggling groups.

Steve ran for the great bulk of the newly arrived PDL 807, his breath rasping in his throat and the pain of his seared and burnt flesh bringing waves of sick agony. A crewman helped him up the loading ramp, and the uniformed captain snapped to a smart salute.

"Commander Edwards at your service, sir. What can I do for you?"

"Blast off!"

"What!"

"You heard me, I said blast off, follow that Vendian ship, the one which fired at the building."

"But sir—"

"Listen you!" Steve tried to be patient but the memory of Harmond's charred body was too recent and painful. "I own this ship, don't I? Then do as I say. Harmond is dead, and I want to get the man who killed him. Blast off! Now!"

"Harmond killed?" Edwards sagged a little, then his white face turned red with anger. "As you say, sir."

He turned and began to snap quick orders, and at his terse command's men sprang about the ship.

"Clear for take-off. Seal hull. Strap down. Ready? Fire!"

Thunder quivered through the great hull, and from the base of the ship fire spouted in savage tongues of searing blue-white flame. The ship trembled, then as the stabbing rocket blast from the gaping venturis reached optimum efficiency, the great vessel jerked and with sudden abruptness headed for the stars. Steve groaned, the acceleration pressure tearing at his weakened body, and desperately he fought to retain full consciousness.

Deep into space the ship drove, following the ion trail of their quarry, tracking the other ship by means of their spent rocket exhaust, and all the time gradually building up speed.

A doctor stooped over Steve and examined his burnt flesh, pursing his lips at the ugly sight of crisped skin and charred flesh.

"Better let me dress those wounds, sir, infection may set in."

"Very well then, but hurry." Steve glanced at the commander. "Sorry to have spoken as I did, but I must catch that other ship. Have we a chance?"

"I think so." Edwards stared at the banked instruments before him and tightened his lips. "We can't travel as fast as I'd like because we have to follow their ion trail, but as soon as they steady on a target-star and engage their nulgrav drive, we can begin to increase our speed."

"Good." Steve winced as the doctor thrust a hypodermic into his arm, then relaxed as the soothing drug blocked the pain sensations from his tortured nerves. "How fast can we go?"

"As fast as any other ship in space, except the Galactic Patrol of course. At least," the commander looked at Steve, "we used to be able to."

"Don't worry about me," smiled Steve understanding the commander's pause. "I'm used to high speed, and the doctors tell me that I'm a perfect physical specimen."

"Have you travelled on nulgrav drive before, sir?"

"No, but I've known acceleration pressure up to twelve gravs for twelve hours."

"Have you!" Edwards glanced at the young man. "Where was that?"

"I entered for one of the cross-system races and gave the ship all it had, the experience was not one that I would repeat unless I had to."

"I see, but the nulgrav effect isn't quite the same as normal acceleration pressure. It isn't easy to describe, but not everyone can stand it."

A light flashed on the instrument panel, and the commander threw a contact.

"Control room here."

"Observation dome to control. Quarry ship has taken to nulgrav drive, the ion trail has dispersed beyond instrument detection."

"What target-star?"

"Sirius."

"That settles it!" Edwards smiled tightly at the young man seated in the dual control chair beside him. "They are heading for Vendis, the whole thing was planned." He hesitated. "What are your orders, sir?"

"Follow them!"

"Yes, sir, but you know that they are armed?"

"I know that, and so are we."

"You mean to blast them, sir?"

"No. I want the man who fired that blast to be brought to trial, but I want that man!"

"Yes, sir, but if they should fire on us?"

"Then we blast them to atoms!" Steve glanced at the set features of the commander. "Is that what you want?"

"I was very fond of Harmond," Edwards said quietly. He glanced at the control panel, then pressed the button of the intercom.

"Control to ship. Stand by for nulgrav drive. Control to observation dome. Watch for quarry vessel. Control to turrets. Stand by for immediate action."

He smiled at Steve. "Ready?"

"Yes."

"Then here we go!" Deliberately the commander operated controls. Unconsciously Steve tensed in the cushioned padding of his chair.

Nothing happened!

Nothing that is except for a mounting metallic whine from the humped bulk of the nulgrav engines, a shrill vibration quivering through the metal of the deck plates and bulkheads and sending little quivers rippling over the flesh as the nulgrav field penetrated every atom of the ship and hull.

Steve hunched forward in the padded chair and tried to hide his disappointment. He had heard so much of the nulgrav drive, had expected so many things to happen, but everything seemed just as before. Edwards smiled at him, guessing from the young man's expression just what he felt.

"Disappointed?"

"A little, I expected…" Steve shrugged. "I don't know what I expected, but not this."

"Wait," promised the commander, "we haven't yet reached the speed of light; when we pass the edge, you'll find out why nulgrav men have to be tough."

"The edge?"

"Yes, that's what we call it, I don't know why." Edwards stared at his instruments and began firing the main drive. A quivering built in the hull, a trembling of metal as the very atoms strained in the encompassing grip of the nulgrav field. They strained to increase their mass, strained and failed and in failing actually decreased it. The un-acquired mass was transformed into sheer energy, led through and past the nulgrav engines and fed into the main rocket drive. The miracle of Cantell's invention was that the faster the ship went, the faster it could go.

Impatiently Steve stared at the blank face of the mass detector screen, waiting for the little fleck of green fight which would register the position of the ship they were following. He stared until his eyes burned, but the screen remained dark, and impatiently he turned to the commander.

"Can't we go faster?"

"Yes, but it takes a little while to build up speed. We can't reach any real velocity until we have passed the edge, then watch us travel!"

Outwards the ship plunged, out past the orbits of Jupiter and Saturn, past Uranus and Neptune, and finally past the far-flung orbit of cold Pluto. Behind them the sun shank into a tiny ball of yellow fight, then a pea-sized coal, then dwindled until it became lost among the glittering glories of the thickly scattered stars.

Edwards grunted and pointed to the instrument-lined panel. "Here it comes! The edge!"

Before them the brilliant star of Sirius seemed to jerk to one side, then split and split again. It blazed a brilliant blue and for a moment Steve could see several stars each identical with the other. Gradually they moved closer together, and finally Sirius blazed before them a glittering point of blue.

"Gets you, doesn't it?" Edwards grinned at the young man. "The colour alters because of the Doppler effect, the same reason why a train whistle seems to sound higher when a train comes towards you than when it has passed. If we looked backwards, the stars would all seem to have become dull and red."

"What made Sirius seem to split and move?"

"That's why we call it the edge, a visual effect caused by breaking a natural law, for some reason we persist in looking for the star at the point where we last saw it, and persistence of vision takes care of the rest." Edwards reached out and again increased the thrust of the main drive.

Steve felt a peculiar sensation race over his body, a skin effect as though he were somehow being inflated and was swelling slightly. He shook his head to clear his ears of a high-pitched ringing noise, and for a moment his eyes seemed as if filled with fog so that it was difficult to see.

"Are you all right?" Edwards glanced at Steve and frowned a little.

"I feel funny… Is that an effect of nulgrav?"

"Yes."

"Ignore it then, increase the speed, we must catch that other ship."

Obediently the commander bore down on the firing controls.

Time passed, a slow dragging eternity of ever-increasing speed. The shrill metallic whine from the nulgrav engines seemed to throb against their very bones and beat against their naked brains. Still the commander increased their speed.

Steve watched the mass detector plate until his eyes ached, and then he stared at the glimmering scene transmitted by the visi-screen. Once he glanced at the commander. Edwards was breathing deeply, his face pale and moist with sweat. A thin trickle of blood ran from his bitten lips but still his hands-were steady on the controls.

A light flashed on the panel, and automatically Steve closed the circuit.

"Observation dome to control. Ion trail detected."

"What density?"

"Minimum."

"Very good." He opened the circuit and glanced at the commander. "We've picked up their trail, increase the speed."

"More?" Edwards bit his lip and glanced down at his hands. From the pores of his skin little drops of blood oozed, mingling with the sweat and staining the controls with red. "Very good."

Steve jerked in his chair as the rockets thrust yet harder against the reducing mass of the hull. Something seemed to burst within his nose and abruptly the scorched leather he wore ran red with blood. He lifted a hand to wipe his face and stared at the red drops oozing from his tender flesh.

"What's happening?"

"We've reached optimum speed, more and it will kill us."

"Are we catching the other ship?"

"I don't know. If we aren't, that crew must be made of iron. Unless we cut gravs soon, we'll die through brain lesions."

Tensely Steve watched the still-dark plate of the mass detector. His body seemed to be on fire, burning with internal pressure as the force of his heart sent the blood oozing from his burst capillaries. Edwards clung half fainting to the controls, his face a mask of blood and sweat, his teeth dug into his bitten lips, his eyes glazed with pain and the dead knowledge of what was happening to them.

Steve fought for breath, sucking in great lungfuls of air, air which seemed to have lost the power to carry oxygen, then he grinned and pointed towards the screen.

A fleck of brilliant green showed bright against the darkness.

CHAPTER SEVEN

Edwards sobbed, his face a twisted mask of agony as he stared towards Steve. His eyes glazed and when he opened his lips a gush of blood rilled down over his chin staining the green and silver of his uniform.

"Cut gravs!" He swallowed painfully and tried to reach the slippery controls. Steve tore his gaze away from the growing speck of green on the detector plate and knocked aside the reaching hand.

"No! We've found them, we can't cut speed now!"

"We must!" The commander gestured towards the firing levers. "We're going too fast—you'll kill half the crew and overshoot the quarry ship. Cut gravs, I tell you! Cut them now!"

Obediently Steve reached for the firing lever and lifted them in their slots. The vibration from the thundering venturis died a little and he eased the controls still more. Their speed died, the nulgrav screen whining with the return of mass and fighting the strained atoms of ship and hull. Edwards breathed more easily then grinned wryly at Steve.

"Man, but we set up a new record then!" He glanced at the banked controls. "That other ship had thirty minutes start on us and operated at maximum velocity all the way. We've caught them up within a parsec, three lightyears, I never thought that men could stand such speed for so long."

"Won't we lose them now that we've cut speed?"

"No. We can afford to lose a little momentum, then track them at a comfortable pace." He stared at the screen, his stained face set and thoughtful. "Well, we've found them Steve, what shall we do now?"

"Take them back." Steve stared at the commander and suddenly grinned. "You have the advantage of me?"

"What?" Edwards looked suddenly uncomfortable. "Sorry, sir, but the commanders have got into the habit of referring to you by your first name."

"I don't mind that, but what's yours?"

"Jack, sir."

"Right, Jack, do I know you?"

"I am the one who found the recording of your father left in space. Mr. Harmond gave me the command of this new ship as a reward."

"Good, now can we radio to that other ship?"

"Not radio, but we can use the sub-etheric impulses." Edwards hesitated. "Better rest up a while first, half the crew must need some sort of attention after that trip, and I could use a wash myself."

"Right, no wait!" Steve stared at the detector screen. "Look, they're slowing down, getting nearer. What—?"

Abruptly Edwards darted his hands over the controls and the great ship jerked to the thrust of straining venturis. From the swollen point of green on the detector screen, other sparks of light had shot, little green flecks spreading in a close-knit pattern from the central point.

"They're firing at us!" The commander stabbed at the attention buttons on the instrument panel before him.

"Attention! Attention! Control to turrets, fire at will!"

Carefully he manoeuvred the ship, veering with sudden bursts of energy from the guiding tubes, and blasting forward with sudden savage bursts of acceleration. The detector screen became filled with darting flecks of green fire and from the gun turrets came a muffled roar as lances of stabbing energy blasted towards the alien ship. Again, Edwards stabbed at the intercom button and snapped quick orders. "Control to radio. Call on sub-etheric impulse beam to that other ship. Order immediate cessation of fire and unconditional surrender." He glanced at Steve his hard features a mask of worry. "They won't pay any attention to us, but we must give them full warning."

"Can we hurt them? The turret guns seem to be useless."

"They're not firing at the ship, but at the neutronium missiles around us. If one should get too near it will heterodyne the nulgrav field and we'll be helpless to manoeuvre."

"Can't we drain the nulgrav field?"

"We can, but if we do we immediately regain mass and lose our momentum, we'd drop to a less-than-light speed and that other ship would simply leave us behind."

"What can we do then?" Steve stared intently at the screen and wished that he could be at the controls. He resisted the impulse to take over. Edwards had what he lacked, experience of the nulgrav ships, experience won the hard way, through actually working the ships over a period of years.

"We must either make them drop their screen or wreck it. While we both are on nulgrav drive, neither can hurt the other. The trick is to do it and remain active ourselves." He stabbed at the intercom button.

"Control to radio. Have you sent that warning?"

"Yes, sir."

"Any reply?"

"None."

"Very well." Edwards closed other circuits. "Control to turrets. How is the range?"

"Too far for energy weapons to be effective."

"Right. Commence firing neutronium bombs. Spread a pattern around them."

"Yes, sir." The click of the opening circuit was followed by the faint vibration from the turrets as the neutronium bombs were fired into space. Harmless things in themselves, yet the terrible mass of the neutronium would be sufficient to overstrain the nulgrav field and force a vessel either to cut the drive or to run the risk of being volatised into incandescent vapour.

Tensely Steve waited, watching the darting flecks of green fire on the mass detector screen. Automatically he felt the distant thrust of the rockets as they veered the ship from out of the path of the deadly missiles being fired at them.

Again, the turrets fired, again and again. All space seemed to be filled with the darting flecks of green, each a terrible hazard to peaceful shipping, and each seeming to miss the target.

Abruptly the end came. Something jarred against their hull, and for a moment the nulgrav engines shrieked with the sudden terrible efforts of holding the field in stasis. External gravitational fields meshed with the nulgrav screen, meshed, and strained to twist the distorted atoms of the hull back into their natural paths. A smell of burning filled the ship, the stench of seared insulation and the bitter electronic tang of released ozone. For one terrible instant it seemed that the field would collapse, that the nulgrav engines would fuse into molten rubbish, then it was over, and the thin metallic whining steadied into its normal drone.

Edwards wiped sweat from his forehead and looked sickly at Steve. "They almost got us, a little more mass—" He fell silent staring dully at his instruments.

"Where is the other ship?" Steve stared at the detector screen his eyes searching the drifting green flecks of the neutronium bombs for the larger point that had been the ship.

"I don't know." Edwards pressed at the intercom button.

"Control to observation. Where is the enemy vessel?"

"Dropped below the edge, sir." The answering voice sounded jubilant. "We hit them with one of the bombs and they lost their nulgrav drive."

"Good. Watch for them."

"We've won then?" Steve slowly clenched his fists. "Now to find the man that murdered Harmond."

Edwards nodded and began to operate the firing levers of the main drive rockets. "We must reverse direction, then cut our drive and let normal mass replacement slow us down." He smiled a little as he watched the flickering needles before him.

"The fortunes of war, Steve. We must have hit them at the same time they hit us. We had the greater normal mass and so were able to absorb the gravitational field of the neutronium bomb. They had a lesser mass, and we were using bigger bombs, they didn't have a chance."

Slowly the great ship lost speed, reversed direction, and beneath the thrust of the flame-spouting venturis, shot back along its previous path. Edwards stared at his instruments, made careful calculations on the electronic computer built into the control desk, and grinned at Steve, one hand resting on a toggle before him.

"Here we go, Steve. I'm cutting the nulgrav drive." Deliberately, he threw the toggle.

Mass flooded back into the vessel. At the speed of light under natural law, an object would have infinite mass, and the ship was travelling at several times the speed of light. It was impossible to have more than infinite mass, the mere statement was a contradiction of terms, and so the ship had to respond to natural law. It slowed almost immediately, slowed to well below light speed, for if it could not have more than infinite mass, neither could it have infinite power. Energy strained throughout the vessel, a strange shivering twisting of the external atoms of flesh and cloth and metal. Little sparkles of energy danced from every point, then faded away as the speed dropped still more.

The whining of the nulgrav engines died, the power needed for the initial operation of the field draining back into the banked accumulators. Stars flashed suddenly around them, the normal stars of a normal universe, glittering and twinkling as the ship jerked and quivered a little as it settled down to yet lower speeds.

Abruptly the rockets thundered through the hull, the long blue-white exhaust stabbing for miles across the void, and Steve sank deep into the cushioned chair beneath the savage thrust of acceleration.

"There!" Edwards pointed to the star-covered visi-screen. "The ship!"

A slender needle-shaped vessel slowly rotated before them, its ports dead and lightless, its hull strangely twisted as if seared by some cosmic force. Starlight glinted from the polished metal of gaping venturis and glittered from the dark ports. In the swollen turrets, the snouting muzzles of guns pointed with empty menace at the distant stars.

"Are they still alive?"

Edwards shrugged and pressed the button of the intercom.

"Control to radio. Contact enemy ship with radio, sub-etheric, and signal lights." He closed fresh circuits. "Control to turrets. Aim at enemy ship and be prepared to fire at any hostile action."

Time dragged as they watched the slowly rotating ship. Then, "Radio to control. No reply to signals."

"That's it!" The commander stared at Steve a question in his eyes. "They are all probably dead, crisped to ash when their field broke beneath the impact of the neutronium bomb. What do you want us to do now?"

"Board her."

"It may be a trap."

"We must chance that." Steve rose from his chair and smiled tightly down at the blood-smeared commander. "I will lead the boarding party, if it is a trap then you can blast the ship to atoms, but I intend getting Harmond's murderer if he is still alive."

Edwards shrugged and began to gently manoeuvre the great vessel towards the crippled wreck—and it was a wreck!

Standing on the outer skin, held by the magnetic attraction of his boot soles, Steve could see the great rips and tears in the twisted hull. He stared at it for a moment, then grimly began looking for the airlock. A tiny voice whispered within the space suit, echoing from the globular helmet.

"I've found the airlock, shall I burn a way in?"

"Wait!" Carefully Steve walked around the hull and joined the other three men of the boarding party. One of them held a portable welding plant, and he gestured with the instrument at the thin crack of the sealed airlock.

"Any reply to your knocks?"

"No, they must all be dead in there."

"Open her up!"

Flame stabbed from the nozzle of the cutting torch and sparks showered briefly from the stubborn metal of the warped hull. Rapidly the man cut around the door, the atomic flame slicing through the adamantine metal as though it were butter. A final flurry of molten sparks, and the door swung open.

"Careful now, the ship may still be airtight."

"I'll run a test hole," grunted the man with the cutting torch. "We don't want to be blown into space from released air pressure." Intently he bent over the brilliant flame.

A thin plume of vapour leapt from beneath the instrument, a tiny thread of white, expanding and condensing to a thin fine snow.

"Still airtight, sir."

"Right. Can you reseal the outer port?"

"Yes, but I'll have to weld it tight, and if anything is waiting for us in there, we wouldn't have a chance if they blasted the inner door."

"I see." Steve glared at the thin inner door and at the expanding thread of condensing water vapour. He winced a little from the pain of his burns, the nerve block had worn off and agony stabbed along his tortured nerves.

"Burn it in!"

"Right!" Rapidly the flame sliced through the thin metal, the white plume of released air expanding and streaming around them covering the bulky space suits with a thin white rime. Steve kicked impatiently at the sagging panel, and abruptly air blasted at them, blasted, then died away.

Grimly Steve led the way into the silent vessel.

It was a ship of the dead! Beneath the dim flicker of their hand beams strange shadows moved, the shadows of twisted metal, warped and curled with the passage of torrents of blasting energy. The nulgrav drive engines were masses of slumped rubbish, the control room a litter of splintered instruments and burnt wiring. Throughout the ship all that remained of the crew, were little piles of ash, rested in distorted positions.

For a long moment Steve stood gazing at the wreckage, absently he stirred one of the little heaps of ash with the metal sole of his boot, then abruptly turned away.

"Back to the ship, we can do nothing here."

"Yes, sir, but—?"

"What is it?"

"This vessel is a hazard, sir. It rests in the space lanes, a danger to any nulgrav ship using this route."

"I know that, well destroy it when we return to the ship."

"If I may suggest a better method??"

"Well?"

"The atomic storerooms are untouched, if we started an atomic fire, the ship would burn itself to harmless ash."

"Very well, do as you suggest." Steve swayed a little feeling the sharp fierce agony of returning pain. "I must get back to the ship. Do your work and return as soon as possible."

"Yes, sir." The man stared at him, his face pressed close to the transparent port of his helmet. "Should one of us return with you, sir?"

"No. I'll be all right, it's just reaction. Get on with your work."

"Yes, sir." The man turned away, the others following him, and Steve watched the darting beams from their hand lights flicker and die as they penetrated deeper into the wrecked vessel.

He felt very tired, his head throbbed, and his eyes seemed to have lost their power to focus properly. He stumbled towards the gaping hole in the hull and stood for a moment swaying beneath the faint attraction of his magnetic boots.

Before him the stars seemed to reel and twist in strange motion, swirling and spinning as if they were diamond chips on a spinning wheel. He stumbled again, tearing the soles of his boots away from the hull, beneath the thrust of his knees drifted gently from the wrecked vessel.

He laughed, jerking his arms, and staring with glazed eyes at the blurring stars. They glimmered, twinkled, and blazed with pure adventure and beckoning promise. They crowded around him, great blazing suns, burning, burning, burning his very body to fine ash, searing his flesh with ghastly heat. Suddenly he screamed with sheer terror.

CHAPTER EIGHT

Silence, and the deep, deep restfulness of a child unborn. Silence, and the crisp wonderful cold of outer space where the distant suns blazed like the scattered jewels of bright adventure. Silence, and the sweet soothing sleep of unknowing innocence.

He slept.

Pain! Pain and the low murmur of muffled voices, the tinkling sound of metal and glass; the sharp stab of needles and the dull searing fire of roasting flesh. Desperately he strove to move, to fight this terrible agony of his dumb body, to give shrieking voice to his ghastly pain.

Footsteps echoed sharply from the distant floor. Someone stood over him murmuring softly through his haze of agony, then something stung his arm, and blackness rose to wrap him with its deep oblivion. When next he awoke the pain had gone.

He rested quietly, staring at the soft green of the ceiling, and hearing the gentle whine of the air-conditioning apparatus as if it were a sound from some other world. He moved a little, and the movement seemed awkward and stiff, and with the return of memory came surging fear.

"My arms!" He almost screamed the words. "My arms! "

Someone moved beside him, and he caught the fragrance of soft perfume.

"Steve! You're awake at last! I'm so glad, Steve. I'm so glad!"

"Madge!" He stared at the girl and tried to smile, but his features felt stiff, and he sunk in the quick return of fear. "What happened to me, Madge? What have they done me?"

"Nothing, Steve, nothing. You've been ill, very ill, for while we thought—" She swallowed and smiled through her tears.

"Never mind that now. You've recovered, and the rest is a matter of time."

"I must know!" He stared at her and tried to rise in the bed. "What happened to me?"

"Lie down, Steve. Lie down!" Gently she pressed him back onto the inflated mattress. "You almost died. You were terribly burnt from the blast which killed my father." She swallowed again and blinked the tears from her eyes. "And then you had to go and almost kill yourself by chasing that ship. Edwards told me how you drove the ship, faster than any other ship has been known to travel, you almost killed three of the crew."

"I didn't know that." He stared at the ceiling and tried to calm his mind. "You haven't told me yet, Madge. What have they done to me?"

"Done to you? Why nothing, Steve." Suddenly she understood and smiled at the worry on his strained features.

"I don't believe you! My arms, I can't move them as should." He forced himself to remain calm. "Tell me, Madge did they amputate?"

"Of course not, Steve. You haven't been fitted with artificial arms."

"Then what happened?"

"You lost almost all of your skin. They had to put you into a saline tank and give you intravenous feeding and artificial oxygenation. You have a new skin, Steve, and naturally it feels tight and uncomfortable. You'll have to have massage and exercise."

"I see." Relief flooded him, leaving him weak and trembling with reaction. "Thank you, Madge. Thanks a lot."

"Rest now, try and sleep. You'll be up within a few days, and there's so much to do, Steve, so much to plan and arrange. We need you, the whole system needs you. Hurry and get well."

"I will," he promised and smiled gratefully as he sank into the soft warm embrace of healing sleep.

* * * *

Madge had spoken but a part of the truth. Steve listened to the delegate of the World Federation and felt his stomach knot as he absorbed the news. He rested on a chair, his body almost healed and his mind as active as before his injuries. The delegate, a small withered old man, trembled is he rustled a sheaf of papers and his thin old voice sounded like the stirring of autumn leaves.

"It's war, Mr. Franson! War! The Vendians have blamed us for the destruction of three of their ships, and they know all about the vessel you chased and wrecked in space. They call it an act of piracy and demand restitution."

"Can't we pay it?"

"No, not even if we wanted to, and frankly, we see no reason to punish you for the episode. From eye-witness reports of the happenings at the space port on Canton, it is clear that the blast from the alien ship was intentional. They knew who would be in that office, and it was sheer chance that you weren't killed with Harmond."

"What do they demand?"

"The surrender of all the ships of Planetoid Disposals Ltd."

"They do?"

"Yes. If we do as they demand it will leave us utterly helpless and at the mercy of Interstellar Salvage Inc. Every one of our nulgrav ships would have to pay tribute to them, or be destroyed in the space lanes, but that is not what the Vendians are after."

"Isn't that enough?"

"More than enough, but they are mad, Mr. Franson. Mad! They have taken everything we had to offer, even the secrets of the nulgrav drive, and now they are turning on us, and upon every intelligent race in the galaxy. They want the sole right of operating the nulgrav ships, they want a monopoly of interstellar trade."

"I see." Steve rose from his chair and strode about the room, feeling the ripple of his muscles beneath his new healed skin.

He stood at one of the high windows, staring out into the night, watching the brilliant glitter of the distant stars.

"How can we beat them?"

"Beat them? Impossible! They have prepared for this, prepared for it ever since we gave them the nulgrav drive. They have ships, hundreds of ships, armed and ready sweep the space lanes the whole width of the galaxy."

"We have ships too," reminded Steve, "and the men to run them. There isn't a nulgrav crewman who wouldn't be with us."

"What good would that do? I tell you that they are armed and ready and willing to destroy. We aren't, and you know it. Earth has outgrown war, our ships are for peace, and are the ships of Planetoid Disposals. We could do some damage, but how much? Our ships must concentrate on protecting trade. They will seek to destroy it, and destruction is always easier than construction."

"What of the Galactic Patrol?"

"I don't know." The delegate slumped in his chair, his thin old features tensed and strained with inner conflict. "We have relied on them for too long, and it was a mistake. We should have had our own war-fleet, but we believed in the intelligence of the Vendians, believed in it too much. Intelligent men do not go to useless war."

"There is something here that I cannot understand." Steve turned from the window and stared at the little delegate. "Why aren't the Vendians afraid of the ships of the Galactic Patrol? What secret have they to make them invulnerable to the Pax Galactica?"

"Need they have one? This coming war is a trade war, a war of pretence. They will 'accidentally' destroy the nulgrav ships. They will apologise, but their ships will haunt the space lanes, and no trader will be safe. Traders will avoid Earth, be afraid to come near us, and like the widening ripple on a pool, so will that fear spread. The nulgrav ships will die, and with them will die the civilisation of man!"

"I know that!" Steve glared at the little delegate his features tight and hard. "Harmond knew it, and my father learned the hard way—he died learning it. What has Earth done all these years?"

"We have backed Planetoid Disposals Ltd., and you are the head of the company now, the largest space fleet in the history of man." The little delegate clutched Steve's arm and stared intently into the young man's eyes. "You are our space fleet!

"We, all of us, look to you to save us. The economy of Earth couldn't stand the cost of a war-fleet, and we relied on the Galactic Patrol. We hoped that you and your fleet would keep the space lanes clear for the nulgrav ships, and we still hope that. Earth isn't weak, not as you think Earth is weak, for you are Earth and your fleet is Earth, and while ours and your fleet still operate the star routes, the Vendians cannot win."

"I hope that you're right," said Steve dryly, "but more than words will be needed." Impatiently he slammed his fist into the palm of his other hand. "What is the Vendians secret? Why have they dropped the mask? Surely, they can't believe that this pretence of a mere trade-war will satisfy the Galactic Patrol? Three times before their ship have come to keep the Pax Galactica, and each time there has been less provocation than this."

"I don't know. For two years now, we have been appealing to the Galactic Patrol—whoever or whatever they are—but we have received no answer. We don't know that they have even received our message." The little delegate stared numbly at the floor, his thin hands trembling as he tried to hide his emotion.

Steve looked at him and felt a momentary contempt. The little man felt fear, terrible soul-destroying fear. Then as he remembered, his expression softened. The World Federation wasn't afraid for themselves, but for all the race of man. They didn't fear for their own safety, but they fought to prevent a new dark age descending on the galactic races.

He dropped a firm hand on the old man's shoulder. "I do my best, and the ships of Planetoid Disposals will do what they can.

We shall arm, atomic torpedoes, heavy duty flare guns; each ship will carry enough destruction to blast a planet to atomic dust. We shall fight fairly while we may. If they confine warfare to the space lanes, then so shall we—but if they drop one single bomb on any inhabited planet, then we shall turn Vendis into atomic ash!"

"Will that help Earth?" The little delegate smiled wearily at the tense figure of the tall young man.

A tiny buzz came from an instrument strapped to his wrist.

"Yes?"

"Report from scouting vessel, sir." The tiny metallic voice had an emotionless quality as it vibrated from the wrist-radio.

"What is the report?" The World Federation delegate raised his wrist so that Steve could hear the reply.

"The Vendians have blockaded their sector of space, sir. They have established a null electronic field and sown space for a light year radius about Vendis with neutronium bombs."

"I see. Have they any vessels guarding the sector?"

"Yes, sir. Powerful armed nulgrav ships, and planetary forts orbiting in three spheres of influence about the planet."

"Very good. Report received and understood." The little man pressed the tiny stud on the wrist-radio and stared grimly at Steve.

"You see how it is?"

"I see." Steve strode impatiently about the room. "They must have prepared for this for years. Orbiting forts, armed vessels, and a null-electronic field!" He stared at the delegate. "How did they establish that field? I have always understood it to be no more than a mathematician's dream, something theoretically possible, but only under circumstances never obtained in normal space."

"I don't even pretend to guess at how they did it. The Vendians have always been imitators; they can take a discovery and improve it, but never have they contributed anything really new. The null-electronic field must have been their one discovery, and the mathematics of that had already been worked out by Cantell."

"Cantell!"

"Yes, you should know of him better than anyone else. He did a lot of work during the past fifty years, and the null-electronic field was part of it."

"Now I begin to understand." Steve stood for a moment wrapped in thought. "I remember his talking of some such thing just before he died. He claimed to have solved the secret of instantaneous transmission. I thought that he was raving, that he had grown weak in the intellect." He laughed curtly. "The old man was saner than any of us; he spoke the cold truth, and we didn't realise what it was he meant."

"Cantell was the greatest scientist the worlds have ever seen, and it will always be a tragedy that he died when did. With his intellect, we might have been able to nullify the field. But now—?"

"Now we get to work!" Steve smiled down at the little delegate. "I want the best minds available, the cleverest electronic technicians, the most experienced atomic theorist! Cantell left papers behind him, masses of scrawled equations, and somewhere in all that scribble are the secrets of both nullifying the null-electronic field and of instantaneous transmission. We must find those secrets, and we must find then before Vendis unleashes the horrors of interstellar warfare!"

"Have we time?" The little man glanced hopefully at the head of the great company. "They are ready for war, and we have to do so much. Have we time?"

"We shall make time." Steve breathed deeply, feeling the freshly healed skin across the muscles of his chest and back stretch and yield to the thrust of his powerful lungs. "Get those scientists. You know what must be done. Let them work at Cantell's laboratory on Canton; they will have everything to hand there and need waste no time."

"I can do that, but what will you do to gain the necessary time?"

"Arm my fleet and engage the enemy. They are taking their time, hoping for a bloodless victory and undamaged spoils. They established their null-electronic field and guarded their planet first; that shows that they still fear the Galactic Patrol, and it also shows that now they think that the Pax Galactica can no longer apply to them."

"Does it? How?"

"The Vendians have dropped the mask. Everything they have done recently has been aggressive, and still the ships of the Galactic Patrol have not appeared to enforce peace. Somehow, the Vendians have discovered a weakness in the Pax Galactica. Somehow, they can afford to ignore it."

"The null-electronic field you mean?"

"Yes, if they have established the field, then they are almost invulnerable. No engine can work within its influence, and no rocket fire—the rockets are ionic and not chemical. The nulgrav drive would fuse into molten rubbish, and even atomic bombs would be as so much useless scrap metal."

"Then what can we do?"

"Attack! Keep their ships within their own sector of space. The null-electronic field must be in the form of a hollow sphere about the planet; they dare not do otherwise, for if they tried to establish it too near the surface, then all machines would stop, all electrical motion cease." Steve frowned in thought. "Their fleet must be outside of the field, and the orbiting planetary forts within it. There must be cleared paths through the neutronium bomb areas, and their nulgrav cargo ships must pass the null-electronic field at set intervals when the field is momentarily collapsed." He smiled a little, a tight hard smile. "We'll coop them up, prevent the cargo ships reaching them, and prevent their space fleet from raiding Earth."

"Will such a plan work?"

"No." Steve stared grimly at the little man. "Such a plan will never win us the war, but it may give us time—time to learn how to defend ourselves from the insane threats of an insane people, and time is what we must have."

"You will lose ships and men, hundreds of ships and thousands of men. Is it worth it? Can't we wait and hope for the Galactic Patrol?"

Steve smiled grimly and slowly shook his head.

CHAPTER NINE

Like giant bubbles of glistening metal, the spaceships rested on the landing field of Canton space port. Dozens of them, their smooth hulls marred by the plastic of newly built turrets heavy with the snouting muzzles of multiple guns. Men stood beside them, tough hard bitten nulgrav crewmen, their faces marred by the thin red streaks of burst capillaries, their eyes cold and hard at the thought of their idle cargo ships and of hampered trade. They stood by their ships—they stared at the glittering stars and ached to get into swift and violent action.

Steve, at the edge of the field, smiled as he saw the resting ships and the ready men. Half of the vessels of his fleet, almost two thirds of the wealth of Planetoid Disposals Ltd were already in space, scattered among the stars on their eternal task of sweeping the space lanes clear of debris. That task must always come first. Of the remainder, half was scouting space against a surprise attack from the Vendian fleet, these few remained as the final barrier between the power of Vendis and the safety of Earth.

Steve shivered a little in the cool night air and stepped towards the waiting flagship.

"Steve!"

He turned and smiled as a girl ran towards him. "Madge! I thought that you were at the laboratories."

"I should be. but I had to see you leave." She clutched at his arm. "Must you go, Steve?"

"I want to, Madge." He frowned as he stared down at her worried features. "The World Federation wouldn't let me command the outer fleet, but I insisted that I should go with this one."

"Please be careful," she begged. "You would be of more use to us in the laboratories helping to unravel Cantell's equations than out in space."

"Perhaps I would, Madge, but I must go." Gently he disengaged his arm. "Take care of yourself, and you can always radio me if I'm really needed."

Grimly he strode towards the waiting vessel, not daring to look behind at the sobbing girl.

One after the other the great ships rose into the glittering heavens, the flames from their rockets searing the burnt concrete of the wide field. Buildings shook beneath the thunder of their passing, and like a cloud of fire-tailed comets they rose to dwindle into the vastness of outer space.

Steve sat in his deeply cushioned chair before the banked instruments and stared at the star-shot blackness before him. They used the thrust of the ion rockets alone, not bothering with the nulgrav drive, and the fierce thrust of acceleration sent a singing through his blood.

Outwards they sped, past the orbit of Mars, through the asteroids, the detector screens flaring as they dodged the litter of a broken planet. Jupiter was left behind and Saturn with its rings illuminated the visi-screens for a moment. Hours passed, long dragging hours of continuous savage acceleration and like an expanding sphere the fleet spread outwards.

A light flashed on the panel before Steve, and he closed a circuit.

"Ships in position, sir."

"Good. Cut rockets and drift. Keep detector screens at maximum overlap."

"Yes sir."

The rockets died, the long blue-white flames of the speeding ions of the exhaust flickered and ceased. With the cessation of acceleration came the nausea of free fall. Men gulped at the retching of their stomachs and hastily swallowed little green tablets of gravinol. They activated the magnetic power of their boots soles and swayed like helpless leaves as they moved slowly about the confines of the great vessels. Steve slumped in his chair and stared at the eternal night of space. Nothing to do now but wait, wait until the invading fleet of the Vendians should sweep towards a defenceless Earth, dropping from faster-than-light speed as they neared the solar system, their guns cleared to destroy a civilisation.

A humming came from the attention signal, and automatically he pressed a button. "Yes?"

"Radio to control. Sub-etheric connection established between flagship and Commander Edwards of the outer fleet."

"Edwards! Connect me."

The sub-etheric screen glowed beneath the pulse of surging electrons, and dimly the strained features of Edwards limned themselves on the screen.

"Steve?"

"Yes, what is it, Edwards?"

"Hell, Steve, sheer hell! They've broken out from our blockade, seven ships, and they've started sheer wanton destruction."

"What do you mean? How is the fleet?"

"The fleet?" Edwards grinned, his twisted features stained and streaked with blood and the greasy smoke of the flare-gun discharges. "Gone, Steve, gone. We did our best but what could we do? They had warships, armoured vessels carrying three guns to our one. We fought, but it was a massacre. The fleet is gone, Steve, gone into atomic dust and twisted metal. Three are left, three out of more than a hundred."

"So soon?" Steve stared at the screen and felt his stomach tighten as he gazed at the far-off commander. The outer fleet gone, totally destroyed, and the Vendians unchecked and heading towards Earth. "Tell me about it," he said tiredly.

"They were waiting for us, and we fell into a trap." Edwards lined features sagged as he made the confession. "We stopped at several planets, and Steve, those worlds had been blasted; they were rotten with radioactive dust. I couldn't believe what had happened. It seemed too wanton, beyond even the Vendians insane cruelty." He paused, and Steve could see the emotion jerking the commander's stained features.

"We headed into position, and just as we dropped from nul-grav drive, they blasted us. We didn't expect it—we weren't really ready for war, and they took us by surprise." He frowned a little as he wiped sweat from his face and neck.

"We fought back, of course, what was left of us. We did damage, terrible damage, all but seven of them either retired or were blasted open, but seven got through, Steve—seven, and any one of them is capable of destroying Earth!"

"Return to the system," snapped Steve sharply.

"No. I'm going to get some of them before I die. Such people shouldn't be allowed to live; not because of what they did to us, we were ready and able to fight back, but because of what they did to the peoples of those seared worlds. There was no need for that, Steve, no need at all."

"Return at once!"

"Not yet, not until I've made the devils pay a little for what they did to peaceful men and women."

"Return, I say!" Steve glared at the screen. "This isn't a private war, man—you are needed here, every ship and man is needed. Return to base. That is an order!"

Edwards hesitated, then yielded with a strange expression in his eyes. For the first time, Steve noticed the charred cloth of the other's uniform.

"As you say, commander." The screen went suddenly dark.

Abruptly Steve pressed buttons on the panel before him. "Attention! Attention! All ships be watchful for enemy vessels. Seven ships are headed towards Earth. Blast on sight. Repeat. Blast on sight!"

He leaned back in the padded chair. He couldn't really blame Edwards for falling into a trap and losing his fleet. Men weren't war-minded; they hadn't practised that art for generations, and it was something learned from hard experience. To never underestimate your enemy, to always be expecting the worse, and to be ready to shoot first and ask questions afterwards, all these things were a forgotten art.

Men had remained peaceful for too long, had relied on others to defend them, and now that the need was here, they were lost in the fog of their own innate decency. To destroy a world was unthinkable. To sear and burn innocent people with the dross of atomic piles was a crime for which there could be no excuse, and yet that very thing had been done.

There should be a punishment to fit such crimes. A punishment fit for animals who walked and spoke and dressed like men, but who were utterly and definitely—*alien.*

Steve shrugged as he stared at the blank detector screen. First catch your rabbit, and then decide what to do with him. Abruptly he jerked upright in the chair, his hands darting towards the controls.

"Alarm! Ships sighted! Action stations!"

Sirens wailed through the ship, and the rockets thundered into sudden strident life. Rapid instructions snapped over the intercom and from the observation dome a continuous rattle of co-ordinates passed to the turrets.

The weapons lifted, began to track the darting invisible shapes from outer space, and belched fire as they flung atomic torpedoes on a path towards the plunging vessels.

Within the ship sudden acceleration pressed each man back into his seat, the drumming vibration of the spouting venturis sending a quivering drone through bone and metal, flesh, and brain. The launching tubes fired again, again, and yet again, the fiery trails of the guided missiles vanishing into mere dots and points of light to be lost among the burning brightness of the stars.

Far in the distance a burst of brilliant energy dimmed the luminaries with its blue-white atomic flame. A second sprouted into sudden life, and then a third, great blossoms of liberated energy each marking the utter destruction of an enemy ship.

Reports came over the intercom.

"Three enemy ships destroyed with guided missiles."

"Vessels of the fleet are concentrating on battle area."

"Enemy ships have slowed and are manoeuvring to avoid atomic torpedoes."

"Guiding impulses are being heterodyned."

"Orders please!"

"Cease firing guided missiles. Detonate those already in space when heterodyning impulses render them uncontrollable. Advance to close quarters and use energy guns."

The ship thrummed to the pulsing of the rockets, and the visi-screens swirled with an ever-changing pattern of stars. Other ships began to close in, the long blue-white flames from their ionic rocket engines stabbing miles across the void. Before them, in the centre of a rapidly closing sphere, the enemy ships tightened their formation and began to hit back!

Green fire stained the surfaces of the detector screen, and violent gouts of eye-searing brilliance flashed and flashed again as deadly torpedoes laden with atomic explosives were harmlessly detonated in space. Tensely Steve gripped his controls, eyes flickering over the instruments before him, as he jerked the ship from the flight paths of the enemy missiles.

From the turrets the energy guns spouted blazing lances of destruction as the gunners tracked the menacing torpedoes and blasted them into dust. In the radio room, men sat with strained features and quivering nerves as they crouched over their instruments, and with delicate fingers broadcast the heterodyning waves to wrest control of the guided missiles from the enemy.

Savage blasts from the rockets slammed the crews of the defending vessels back into their padded chairs, sending blood streaming from noses and ears and blurring overstrained vision. It seemed as if all space was one mad confusion of searing energy and liberated destruction. A ship exploded into incandescent vapour, torn and volatised by a direct hit. Another jerked, then, with all rockets spouting at full power, sped into the far distance. Yet another spun helplessly beneath the combined fire of two enemy vessels, spun, and drifted dark and lifeless towards the distant sun. Steve tightened his lips and stabbed at the intercom button.

"Combined assault," he snapped. "We've got to get those ships and get them quick. All vessels advance at high speed and with all guns at full blast. Now!"

Grimly he depressed the firing levers, and within the ship the thundering vibration of the main drive thrust at the strapped down crew with savage force. Stars reeled as the ship veered to a new flight path, veered then steadied beneath the thrust of the flaring exhausts. Before them four strange ships grew into rapid nearness.

They were strange ships, of a pattern never-before-seen in a peaceful galaxy. Long and slender, with swollen turrets at nose and stern. The gaping mouths of launching tubes lined their sides, and their hulls were blistered and protected with ridged and corrugated fins. Warships!

Fire stabbed from their multiple guns. Long ravening lances of searing energy, blue-white with the fury of atomic power, stabbed towards the advancing ships of the defending fleet. Steve felt a momentary doubt as he saw them. What chance had a converted peace-time vessel against ships designed for war? He swallowed his doubts and snapped brief orders into the intercom.

"Fire torpedoes. Fire all guns at will. All ships blast with everything you carry. Now!"

From the turrets, a thin black greasy smoke began to seep into the ship, the fumes of discharging weapons. It crawled past the air-tight doors and stained the smooth hull with a thin film of black. It settled on the faces of the crew, on the dials of-instruments, a layer one molecule in thickness, yet covering the interior of the vessel as if it had been electroplated on.

Before the advancing ships, the stabbing fire from the guns dimmed the stars and the distant fire of the sun. It thrust towards the waiting enemy, blasting lances of atomic destruction and mingled with the eye-searing fire slender torpedoes sped silently and invisibly towards their targets.

The enemy struck back!

The hull of the ship quivered, and metal squealed as blasting forces sought to smash and rend. Steve shook the blood from his eyes and grimly drove the vessel directly towards the menacing shapes of the enemy. Fire blossomed to his right, more fire sprang into sudden fury below him, as two of the attacking vessels burned in swift defeat, but they did not go unavenged.

Beneath the concentrated hail of fire from the superior numbers of the defending fleet, the enemy wilted and shrank. Two of the ships exploded simultaneously, the wash of flame from the suddenly liberated energy from their atomic engines blasting a third into a spinning rotation from which it could not recover. Three guided missiles slammed into the helpless vessel, and again all space seemed to be lit with the burning fires of destruction.

Abruptly the single remaining vessel blasted towards the sun. Steve stared at it with sick eyes as he sought to bring his speeding vessel into control. He spun the ship on its axis with screaming gyroscopes and desperately flung the full power of the main drive into the spouting fire of his venturis. Pressure slammed down at him, tremendous pressure, and slowly the ship lost some of its tremendous speed. It slowed, halted its headlong flight from the sun, and began to blast after the sole surviving enemy vessel.

A light flashed before him, and a man's strained voice echoed over the intercom. "Observation to control. That enemy ship has adopted a flight path which will bring it directly to Earth."

"I know that!" Steve tensed over his controls. "We must get that ship before they radi-dust the planet." He stabbed at the attention button. "Attention! Attention! Prepare for nulgrav drive." Without listening to the startled protests from the gasping crew, he engaged the drive and flung the full power of his straining rockets in a desperate bid to beat the fleeing ship.

Sound began to throb throughout the vessel. A thin high-pitched whining, a murmur of overstrained engines, and a thin faint vibration of atoms resisting unnatural stress. Before him, the sun suddenly contracted into a tiny circle, a pea-sized ball, then abruptly began to swell like a balloon. Sound began to echo from the intercom, the half-crazed sounds of a man in terrible fear.

"Cut the nulgrav drive, you fool! We're too near mass, too near the system, the planets, the asteroids. Cut it, I tell you, before we're all twisted and roasted to dust!"

Steve grinned without humour as he half-listened to the engine-room supervisor, but the man was right. They we're far too near bodies of high mass to use the drive. At any moment, the field could collapse, and with that collapse would come inevitable death.

Suddenly he cut the nulgrav drive. For a moment space seemed to flicker around them, alarm sirens wailed through the ship, and the detector screen blazed with green fire. Something grew with terrible speed on the flickering visi-screen, something long and slender and bristling with guns. The long fingers of its rocket exhaust seemed to stab at them, then it was gone, and the great ship reeled to a mighty impact.

Air hissed from torn and ruptured plates, then stilled as automatic bulkheads sealed off the punctured sectors. From somewhere in the vessel, a man whimpered with pain and shock; another swore in a low monotone. Steve sighed and let his hands fall listlessly from the controls.

Beneath them, the enemy ship drifted like a smashed tin can, drifted lifelessly towards the fires of the sun.

CHAPTER TEN

Alarm lights flashed on the instrument panel, a flickering mass of red warning, and the intercom echoed to a man's whispering voice. "Radio to control. Message from the laboratories on Canton."

"Wait!" Steve pressed buttons. "Control to ship. Assess damage." He sat stiff-faced as the reports came in.

"Hull ripped in lower sector, three men dead."

"Number three gun-turret smashed, all crew dead."

"Number two turret torn, all crew alive."

"Observation dome airless."

"Engine room airless."

"Ship operating, but unfit for action."

"Repair what you can. We are going to return to base." Steve reconnected the radio room. "Control ready to take message."

The telescreen swirled with shifting colour and a pale strained face stared at him from the illuminated plate. "Steve!"

"Madge, are you alright? Why are you calling?"

"Trouble, Steve. The scientists have managed to unravel some of Cantell's equations, but some of them don't seem to make sense. They want you to hear so that you can tell them what the old man meant."

"How can I?"

"I don't know, Steve." Madge smiled as she stared at him. "They seem to think that as you were closer to him than any other man, he may have told you something that will give them the key to his scribblings. When can we expect you?"

"I don't know."

"Is anything wrong?" Worry darkened her eyes as she stared at him. Steve smiled reassuringly.

"The ship is damaged a little, nothing to worry about, but repairs will take a little time." He frowned down at the control. "If it is really urgent, better send a ship for me. Send a ship in any case, we have injured men aboard."

"Damaged!" Madge stared at him. "The enemy?"

"Yes." Steve deliberately snapped the brief reply. "Tell me, Madge. Have you heard from Edwards?"

"No, Steve." She looked at him, her eyes searching his face. "What happened?"

"Seven of the enemy penetrated to the system. Edwards had warned us what to expect, and we met them as they dropped from nulgrav drive." He forced himself to smile. "We got them, Madge, all seven of them. The last of them is drifting towards the sun."

"I see, and what are our losses?"

"I'm not sure, but I believe that we lost two for their one. Edwards' fleet has been wiped out. I ordered him to report back to base as soon as possible. Has he had radioed in at all?"

"No, Steve, I haven't heard from him." Madge stared at him her cheeks pale with despair. "The fleet gone! Then if they try to destroy Earth, we have no defence, no defence except the scientists and Cantell's equations. You must return to the laboratories, Steve. You must!"

"Steady," warned Steve. "I'll be there as soon as possible. In the meantime, try and contact Edwards." He smiled. "Goodbye Madge. Take care of yourself." He opened the circuit on her reply.

* * * *

Repairs took little time. What had to be done was done, and the rest of the damage would have to wait until the ship could return to the shipyards.

Steve transferred to a swift inter-system vessel and looked back at the crippled hull of the flagship as they accelerated towards Canton. The great vessel was almost a wreck; the force of the impact with the armoured warship had ripped and torn the adamantine metal of the hull and strained the internal structures. It was doubtful whether the great vessel would ever travel space again.

He arrived at Canton hours later. The laboratories seemed a hive of activity. Men stood tensely over the softly purring computers, trying to make sense out of the streams of figures and scribbled equations left by Cantell. Weston, Master Scientist and one of the foremost theoretical mathematicians, looked helplessly at Steve as he gestured towards a heap of crumpled paper.

"Cantell couldn't have known that he was to die so soon, though the doctors had given him warning enough. These papers he left are almost senseless. If it wasn't for the fact that I knew the old man and knew that he was no fool, I'd be ready to swear that all these equations are a meaningless jumble."

"Whatever they are, they're not that." Steve slumped down into a chair and rested his head in his hands. He felt deathly tired, the long battle, the nerve-wrenching strain of the chase, and the following reaction had left him limp and lifeless. He forced himself to lift his head and begin looking through the papers.

"Are these the ones he had on his bed when he died?"

"No. These were found in his workroom."

"Where are the others? The ones he wrote on when bedridden?"

"I don't know." Western looked at Steve anxiously. "Would they be important?"

"They would." Steve tried to clear his throbbing head. "He was working until the end, and I think we can assume the final products of his work would have been those." The young man smiled at painful memory. "He wouldn't have died without completing his task; the old man was stubborn enough to have held out against death itself until he had finished. Only having finished, would he have yielded the struggle."

Steve paused, thinking of the past. "I was with him when he died, and he was certain that he had solved the secret of instantaneous transmission. He said—he told me—" Steve frowned and bit his lips in thought.

"What did he say? Did he tell you where the final equations were?"

"No, that wouldn't have been necessary—he would have assumed that I'd know. No, it was something else, something important enough for him to have waited to die until he had told it to me." He looked at the old scientist and suddenly smiled with quick relief. "I remember now! He said something about electrons, that everything depended on the electron, that each and every electron was exactly the same as any other electron anywhere. Does that help at all?"

"Yes, it does. We have been working on his new theories of quantum mechanics and sub-space eddy currents. If he was convinced that his discovery was wholly connected with the electron, then we can limit the field of search." The old scientist almost ran from the room in his haste to commence the search for the mislaid papers.

Steve smiled a little and suddenly clutched at the table as the room seemed to reel and sway. Footsteps echoed towards him, and a soft hand smoothed his perspiring forehead.

"Drink this, Steve."

Something acrid and nauseating to the taste filled his mouth and automatically he swallowed and swallowed again. The drink brought quick relief, and he smiled at the strained features of a girl.

"Thank you, Madge. I must have been nearly exhausted."

"You were." She stood looking down at him, a strange expression on her fresh young face. "Steve!"

"Yes, Madge?"

"Steve, I—!"

"What is it? Has Edwards called on the sub-etheric impulses?"

"No!" She seemed unnecessarily sharp, and Steve looked at her in quick anxiety.

"Is anything wrong, Madge?"

"No, nothing that you would call wrong anyway."

"No?" He smiled at her and rose from the chair. "I am not quite a fool, dear," he whispered softly. "You must know that you mean a lot to me, quite a lot, but I daren't speak of that."

"Why not, Steve?"

"It is no secret that your father wanted us to be married. If we had, it would have made him very happy. You know that."

"Yes."

"Then can you understand how I felt about it? I love you, Madge. I think that I've always loved you, but I wanted you to love me in return and not agree to marry me merely to please your father."

"You wanted that." Suddenly she began to laugh, a startlingly human burst of gentle amusement. "Didn't you know that I love you, too, and that I've felt exactly the same as you? You were always so cold towards me, my dear, so distant, and I'd almost given up hope. Steve, must we wait any longer?"

"To marry? Yes, my dear, I'm afraid that we must."

"Why, Steve? Why?"

"Because there is work to do, hard and dangerous work. Planetoid Disposals Ltd. is the greatest company in the history of the solar system, perhaps of the galaxy. Our franchise gave us unlimited power over the uninhabited worlds of space, and we virtually own entire planetary systems, almost you could say, we own Earth. That carries a tremendous responsibility with it. If we own planets, then we are owned by them, too. We must seal an everlasting galactic peace before men can work and build and live in happiness, and until that day, our marriage must wait."

"It may be years, decades!" Madge turned from him, hiding her tears.

"No, Madge. We either win or lose this battle in a very short time. We have until the enemy can re-muster another fleet, and then either Earth flames in atomic disruption, or the Vendians are annihilated. There can be no other peace."

"Destroy a world?"

"Yes." He stood, gripped her shoulders, and turned her to face him. "I know how you feel about it, Madge. I have felt the same way, but there is nothing else we can do. Earth must be strong if we are to survive, strong enough to overcome moral scruple and strike a final blow for freedom. It isn't just Earth, Madge, other worlds have felt what it is to be conquered by the Vendians. Edwards reported that he swept near to planets that had been radi-dusted, wantonly destroyed by the forces of Vendis. No, Madge. They have judged themselves, and they must pay their own penalty."

"Annihilation!"

"Yes." Steve looked over as Weston came bustling into the room. The old scientist was smiling, and he chuckled at Steve's inquiring look.

"We've found them, the papers I mean, and you've put us on the right track." He sat at the table and rubbed his eyes.

"I must be getting old," he grumbled, "my eyes are tired, and I haven't done more than twenty hours work yet."

"Why not get some rest," suggested Madge.

"Rest? Nonsense!" The old man straightened his curved shoulders. "Why, when I was a young man, I often worked two or three days nonstop to finish a line of research. Rest! Sleep is for the old men, the weary, not for me." He rubbed his eyes again. "I wish that my eyes wouldn't burn, though."

"Have you solved the problem?"

"Solved it?" The old man looked at Steve. "You must be joking!"

"No, I'm not joking. Have you solved it?"

"Of course, we have—on paper: but there is a tremendous difference between mathematical theory and actual practice."

"How long will it take—to make a ship based on the new principles, I mean?"

"How long?" Weston shrugged. "Who knows?"

"I must know, and it must be soon." Steve strode impatiently about the room. "This discovery is our sole hope. Either we build a new ship capable of penetrating the null-electronic field, or we watch while Earth burns to atomic ash. Speed man! Speed! We must have speed!"

"I know what you mean but talking about it won't make it any easier. I tell you that we can't build a new ship incorporating the new discovery, it just isn't possible!"

"Why not?"

Weston sighed and looked down at his thin withered hands. "Can you understand, can any man who is not a scientist? The jet engine is a simple thing, one of the simplest devices known, merely a tube with a double set of interior fans. One set compresses air, the other is driven by the expanding gases to provide power to drive the compressor fans. A simple thing, a jet engine, but it took more than thirty years before the theory became workable."

"Thirty years!"

"Something like that; my memory isn't too good on ancient history, and it was long ago."

"What took the time?"

"Technical engineering. Before the jet motor could be successfully built, special metals had to be developed, high temperature alloys discovered, and the whole science of astronautics established before the jet engine, and with it supersonic flight, could be an actual reality. Between some obscure scientist stating that such and such a thing would work and the building of the actual thing, time must always elapse. Sometimes, as with the nulgrav drive, the time is only a few years; at others, it can be decades."

"We haven't got that sort of time."

"I know, but there is nothing we can do to shorten it."

"We must!" Steve clenched his hands into fists. "We've got to! Somehow, we must beat the Vendians, our lives, the whole future of Earth depends on it!" He spun towards the door as an orderly burst into the room. "What is it?"

"Contact with a ship of the outer fleet, sir. Commander Edwards is on the screen by sub-etheric impulse radio."

"Good." Steve raced after the orderly through the busy rooms to the radio shack. He grinned at the features of the commander framed on the flickering plastic of the sub-etheric screen, then stiffened his features into a frown.

"I told you to return to base." he snapped. "Why have you disobeyed my orders?"

"Did you destroy the Vendian ships?"

"Yes."

"Good!" Edwards smiled and relaxed. He wiped grime from his face and neck and grinned at Steve.

"Where are you?"

"About half a light year from Earth."

"You should be here soon then." Steve tried to remain stern, then grinned in surrender. "It's good to see you again, Jack. When will you land?"

Edwards opened his mouth to reply, but suddenly the screen flickered and went dark. From outside came a terrible noise— the noise of men shouting, of sirens wailing, of delicate electronic equipment heterodyned by an immensely powerful carrier wave, overriding normal radio impulses and echoing from every speaker and telescreen in the solar system.

Frantically Steve tried to re-establish radio contact with the vessel speeding towards Canton, tried and failed. A radio operator shrugged as he snapped quick orders and helplessly spun his dials.

"I can't help it, sir. Every carrier-wave on the band is the same. Something is dampening out all our impulses." He looked at the tall young man. "It has happened before, you know, sir."

"Before?"

"Yes, sir. Three times now."

"You mean—" Steve stared at the man, then abruptly lunged for the door. He ran across the small landing field and into the compact observatory. A technician stood by the eyepiece of a fifty-inch reflector. He looked up, startled, as Steve brushed him aside.

Delicately the young man swung the instrument, spinning the cupola on its well-oiled gimbals and aligning the long barrel of the telescope on a certain sector of the heavens. Finally satisfied, he looked, sighed, and looked again.

Hovering one hundred thousand miles from Earth hung a vessel of the Galactic Patrol,

CHAPTER ELEVEN

It was a tremendous vessel, even from this distance Steve could sense the utter immensity of it. A great sphere formed the central portion, a sphere from which two great cones speared diametrically into space, each cone twice as long as the diameter of the central sphere. A faint radiance pulsed over the vessel, a shimmering curtain of pale blue fire, seeming to cling to the hull and writhing as if it were water or some kindred fluid.

"The Galactic Patrol!" Steve felt the stirring of sudden relief deep within him. A similar such ship would even now be hovering above Vendis, threatening utter destruction by its mere presence, a colossal menace against which no single civilisation could ever hope to stand. He sighed as he stared through the eyepiece of the telescope and felt his weariness drain away as he gratefully surrendered the responsibility of protecting a system from his shoulders to the great ships of the Galactic Patrol.

The war was over, the Pax Galactica again ruled the lives and guarded the welfare of mankind!

The technician tugged at his arm and reluctantly Steve turned from the telescope.

"What is it?"

"The radio, sir. The radio—"

Steve frowned, and dimly from an adjoining room, he heard the muffled thunder of a mighty voice.

"It's just the routine warning," he said. "You know, 'be good boys or else', it doesn't apply to us, the Vendians are the ones to worry."

"No, sir." The technician looked scared, his pinched features white and drawn. "I know what you mean, sir, I heard the last warning when the Galactic Patrol came before, but this is different."

"Different?" Steve stared at the man and felt something knot deep within him. "What do you mean?"

For answer, the technician opened the door, and sound flooded around them.

"...therefore, we give you this vessel." A click and the voice began again. "We of the Galactic Patrol, guardians of men and avengers of destruction, have a message for the inhabitants of this solar system, called man. We have failed. We can no longer prevent war and are unable to guard you; therefore we give you this vessel."

Steve stared at the hidden mouth of the speaker, and once again the mighty voice roared its message of doom and forlorn hope. He swallowed, then abruptly switched off the radio.

"What's happened to them?" The technician stared at the tall young man his eyes huge in the paleness of his face. "They always helped us before—why can't they help us now?" Angrily, Steve thrust the man aside as he headed at a run towards the laboratories. Madge gave him a hopeless glance as he burst into the room, and Weston stared at him from his red-rimmed eyes.

"Did you hear the broadcast?"

"Yes." Madge crossed the room and rested her hand lightly on his arm. "Is this the end, Steve?"

"No!" He stared at her refreshed by the sight of her sweet charm, then glanced at the old man. "Weston. As far as I can make out, they are giving us the ship. We all know that the Galactic Patrol have the secret of instantaneous transmission, and that is the one thing we want to beat the Vendians. Well, we have it. The Galactic Patrol have given it to us. All we need do is to take their gift and use it—against Vendis."

"Perhaps." The old scientist stared at the tall young man. "That ship is alien, Steve, remember that. We still need time—time to learn how to operate the controls."

"Maybe." Steve crossed the room and began snapping swift orders into the intercom.

"Landing field? Get the fastest ship you have at hand, ready for immediate flight." He stared at the others. "Weston, select a group of your scientists for examination of the alien ship. Madge, you wait here, and when Edwards arrives, ferry him out to the vessel. Ready?"

They nodded, the old man already selecting his group with rapid stabs of his gnarled forefinger. Hastily they gathered up their papers and charts, their tables and delicate instruments.

Within thirty minutes, they were on their way to the tremendous vessel of the Galactic Patrol.

* * * *

It was huge! The little spaceship seemed to be dwarfed by the tremendous hull. From one tip to the other, the great vessel must have been two miles in length, and the diameter of the central sphere nearly half a mile. Steve stared at the vessel, noticing the swirling ripple of the pale blue fire and feeling a sensation of utter alienness.

A port gaped suddenly before them, and with a wry shrug of his broad shoulders, Steve sent their little vessel drifting through the opening and into the hull.

He jockeyed the rocket blasts of the ship, steering the little craft along a brilliantly lit corridor and then settled it to rest on the metal floor. Startled, he glanced at the instruments, then stared at the old scientist.

"There is air in here, breathable air!"

"Are you certain?" The old man leaned across the cushioned pilot's seat to squint at the instruments. Steve nodded.

"Yes, I noticed the rocket-flare as we landed."

For a moment the closely grouped men sat in silence, then Steve rose from the chair. "I'm going outside."

"Wait!" The old scientist glanced at the others. "Is it safe?"

"It must be. After all, they—whoever they are—gave us this vessel. I cannot see that we have anything to fear from them. They have acted as guardians of the peace for too long for us to doubt them. Well?" He stared at the others. "Are we going, or do we just sit here like frightened children?"

Silently the others followed him, followed him through the airlock and out of the little vessel onto the metal of the deck plates of the alien ship. It was deathly quiet. Nothing broke the silence, not even the whisper of distant machinery or the small sounds of a living ship. For a moment, Steve wondered whether he was living in a dream, so alien it was.

He led the way along the corridor, his feet ringing slightly from contact with the metal of the floor, and from the passageway they entered a great circular room. It was empty, bare of instruments or other furnishings, a great domed chamber, windowless, lit by soft radiance from some hidden source, and warm with half-felt currents of sweetly scented air.

"I don't like this," whispered a man. He glanced nervously over his shoulder. "Where is the crew?"

Someone coughed behind them, and they turned to find a man! He looked like a man, like a very old man with white hair and simple robes and a welcoming smile. He stared at them, then addressed himself to Steve.

"You are the leader?"

"I am."

"Please sit."

The tall young man glanced around him and automatically sat down on a comfortable bench. He didn't feel surprised at its sudden appearance, he felt that he wouldn't be surprised at anything happening in this strange ship. The others joined him on the bench, and the strange old man smiled.

"Of course, I am not as you see me," he said calmly. "You must have guessed that, but the parasympathetics have robbed you of all fear and anxiety. This is essential, for you must believe what I have to say, and fear and belief do not go together."

"You speak our language," said Steve. "How?"

"I do not speak any language," corrected the old man. "I do not speak at all. You are receiving my thoughts by telepathic transference, and yet so indoctrinated are you to the usage of spoken words, that you delude yourselves into believing that you are merely hearing me speak. Enough of that, time presses and there is much that you must learn."

"Yes?"

"The Pax Galactica has ended, the Galactic Patrol can no longer keep the peace." The stranger stared at them and seemed to tighten his lips. "Eons ago, before your race sprang from the mud and slime of your planet, the Guardians ruled the stars and the spaces between the stars, and their rule was good. Time passed, time measured by the passing of suns, and the Guardians grew tired of what they had. Immortal, invincible, physically perfect, and with the whole universe explored and known, they grew bored. They left, they ventured into realms unknown—into a region between the dimensions—and they left us behind to guard the peace of the galaxy. For age upon age we have kept that peace, kept it until now, until one race, more vicious than the rest, discovered the one thing able to defeat us—the null-electronic field."

"The Vendians!"

"As you say, the race of beings inhabiting a planet which they have named, Vendis. Against these people we are helpless, and having once being proved of no further use, we also must depart."

"I see. And what of us?"

"To you we give this vessel, and others like this vessel. They will arrive when and if you solve your problem. To you, we give the Galactic Patrol, and the trust of keeping the Pax Galactica—if you are able to survive."

"Why us?" Steve shifted on the soft bench. "Why the race of man?"

"Because of all the intelligent races of the galaxy, you are the most suitable, the most moral, and the most to be trusted with this responsibility. We are going to join our masters. To you we leave the guardianship of the universe."

"I see." Steve stared at the old man. "I begin to grasp the concept of what you are telling me, but all this must wait. We are engaged in a war the outcome of which will be utter destruction for one or other of two races. We have little time. How can we defeat our enemy?"

"I do not know."

"Tell me, it has long been surmised that these ships have the power of instantaneous transmission. Is that a fact?"

"It is."

"Then why cannot you blast Vendis to atoms?"

"We can, but then also we cannot." The old man seemed to smile as he noticed their wondering looks. "Morally, we are unable to destroy that world. In short, they have called our bluff. We could slowly destroy them by a long term war of attrition, but they would inflict terrible damage on innocent worlds during that time. The null-electronic field is a barrier which we cannot pass, and they have done the one thing which renders them beyond our control. They have defied us to do our worst, and our worst is merely to threaten. We cannot, literally cannot, destroy a world."

"By that do you mean that all this armament is useless?"

"No, but we are unable to destroy."

"I see." Steve smiled in sudden relief. "But we can. We can take this vessel to the edge of Vendis and blow that planet to dust!"

"Yes, but then you could always do that with your own ships."

"How?" Steve frowned as he stared at the old man. "They can stop us using the nulgrav drive. We could never get there by normal means, and even if we did, their null-electronic field would render our weapons harmless. With instantaneous transmission, we could arrive before they knew we were coming, blast the planet, and escape back to Earth ready to defend the system against any ships of their fleet which had managed to escape the destruction of the planet. Without it we are helpless, but this ship has it, why then cannot we use it?"

"The instant-drive, as we may as well call it, is limited in its operation. We can traverse space without loss of normal time, but we cannot materialise within a certain distance of a certain mass. In that the drive is similar to your own nulgrav engines. The barrier around the planet of Vendis prevents materialisation within a tremendous distance and effectively prevents the use of any weapons."

"Is that all?" Steve smiled as he glanced at the old man. "We can overcome that difficulty. Materialise and blast through their fleet and into their world. The null-electronic field is spherical in shape; our weapons would work near the surface."

"A good plan." The stranger seemed to smile at the young man. "Almost it would work, but for one thing."

"What is that thing?"

"Men cannot use the instant-drive. They are not suited to it, and it is very doubtful whether they could stand it. I firmly believe that they would die."

"That is a chance we must take." Steve stared at the old man, and his eyes narrowed in sudden suspicion. "I don't understand this. You say that men cannot use the instant-drive?"

"I do."

"Then how do you retain life? You are a man, the crew of this ship are human, even though your physical shape may not be as ours. You are made of protoplasm, you have blood, bone, nerves and a brain. What you can do, we can do also."

"No." The old man seemed to shake his head. "You make an error."

"Do I?"

"Yes, you see—we are not men."

"Are you not flesh and blood?"

"No, we are not even that. We are nothing composed of what you consider flesh and bone, we are—"

Abruptly the old man seemed to dissolve, to writhe and churn in a ripple of ever-changing form and colour. For a moment horror stood before them, and then—metal gleamed, metal and the crystal of lenses.

They stared at a robot.

CHAPTER TWELVE

"So, these vessels are staffed with robots." Edwards shook his head as he stared about the great circular chamber. "Machines to run machines. It seems unbelievable."

"No, it really makes very good sense." Steve smiled at Madge and gently touched her hand. "What else could keep an aeon-old peace but machines? They don't die, they cannot to be swayed by greed or fear, they merely react to certain stimuli, and in that they have their weakness."

"Weakness?"

"Yes. They must follow a plan, the plan built into them by the long-gone guardians. If ever something happened to break their conditioning, then they are helpless. They cannot make new decisions, that is why the Pax Galactica has broken down, the Vendians refused to fit into normal channels, and the Galactic Patrol is helpless."

"The Vendians!" Edwards rose to his feet and impatiently strode about the great room. He looked tired, tired from his long journey and his eyes were bloodshot and streaked with the thin red lines of burst capillaries. Together with Madge he had arrived at the strange ship shortly before and as yet hadn't been able to rest.

"I captured one of their ships, Steve. It was a crippled wreck and all the crew but one were little piles of charred ash. I took him, and he talked." For a moment something savage peered from the commander's tired eyes.

"The blue devil was dying, his brain ruined by lesions from burst capillaries, and his injuries made him careless. Either that, or he just didn't care what he told me."

"Sit down, Jack." Madge caught hold of the commander's arm. "Sit down and tell Steve about it."

Wearily Edwards slumped into a chair. "After the fleet had been blasted from space, and after you had ordered me to return to base, I hung around for a while." He smiled at Steve. "You can court martial me if you like, but I just couldn't return, not until I had done something to avenge all those people on the wasted planets. I found a ship, a straggler it must have been, and blasted it with every weapon still working on my vessel." He paused, re-living the clash and fire of interstellar battle.

"We forced them to drop their nulgrav field and boarded the enemy ship. As I told you, all were dead but for the captain." Edwards paused, his hands twitching as he thought about the recent past. He stared at them and abruptly thrust them into his pockets. He tried to grin, and Madge shuddered at the look of naked hell on the commander's features.

"They have recalled all their ships, Steve. They have gathered them on Vendis, refitting them with new and terrible weapons, weapons capable of turning a sun into a nova, a planet into a pinch of ash. They are waiting until all their fleet is ready, and when it is they will sweep through the galaxy on a mad orgy of conquest. They cannot be halted once they blast from their native world, the size of their fleet is incredible, every man and woman on the planet, every factory and machine has been channelled into full war production. Vendis is an arsenal, Steve, an arsenal brimming with ships and crews, with atomic explosives and radioactive dusts."

"Was the captain lying?" Steve tightened his lips as he stared at Edwards. "Could he have merely been trying to frighten you with an empty boast?"

"No." The commander shook his head. "I thought of that, had tested him with a lie detector; he was speaking the truth as he knew it. He felt quite safe in telling me what he did, for no man living knows the secret of the null-electronic field and behind that field they are safe."

"Wait a moment!" Steve frowned at the sagging figure before him. "We know that they have the field, the orbiting forts and the neutronium bomb minefields. Have they recalled the guarding vessels from around the planet?"

"No. They have concentrated on defence. From what I heard, it would be impossible for any vessel to get within half a light-year of Vendis without being blasted to dust. The neutronium-bomb minefield would collapse the nulgrav field, and then the guarding vessels of their defence fleet would blast it to ashes. Even if we did penetrate the minefield, the null-electronic screen would render our ships and weapons useless. We would be blasted by the orbiting forts." Edwards shook his head and suddenly slumped lower in his chair. Steve glanced at Madge and gestured towards the unconscious commander.

"Take care of him, will you, dear. I must have a conference with Weston. Time is running out, and there is too much still to be done."

The old scientist looked impatiently at Steve and frowned down at a complex wiring chart before him. He hesitated, then angrily left his work and crossed the busy room to where the tall young man waited for him.

"What is it now?" Weston glared at Steve and looked to where the humped bulk of mighty engines almost filled the room.

"I must talk with you." Steve smiled at the old man and gently drew him through a doorway. "I know that you are eager to solve some new mystery of science, but that must wait, survival comes first."

He led the way back into the great central chamber and forced the old man into a chair. "Now tell me, has your research met with success?"

"Success!" Weston shrugged. "It all depends on what you mean by that word. Thanks to the previous work done by Cantell, we know how instantaneous transmission can be made to operate. The theory is basically simple, and as Cantell told you, it depends solely on electron-mechanics. But knowing how a thing can be done is far different from actually doing it."

"Don't fence with me, Weston!" Steve glared at the old man and forced himself to restrain his impatience. "Words are pleasant things, but we have no time for mere words. How can we destroy Vendis?"

"I don't know."

"Why not?"

Weston sighed and stared helplessly at his questioner, glanced down at his hands, then seemed to sag a little in his chair. "Listen, Steve, and try to understand. This ship contains the instant-drive, but the size of the vessel is solely determined by the drive itself. The robots have been teaching us, and I tell you this, no ordinary ship could ever contain more than a fraction of the essential machinery. Once you know the theory of the drive, the hard facts become only too obvious."

"Well?"

"Look at it this way, Steve." The old man crumpled a sheet of paper into a ball and threw it on the table. "Look at that piece of paper, it is composed of atoms, electrons moving in certain orbits at a certain time and in a certain relationship to each other. Now, if we could reproduce those circumstances exactly elsewhere, what would happen?"

Steve stared at the paper his forehead creased in thought "I begin to understand," he said slowly. "If by some means it were possible to force electrons into exactly the same orbits as those of that paper, then we would have two balls of paper, one here, and one where the focused fields of our forced electrons met. Reproduce the same circumstances, and the same effect must occur, in this case, a piece of paper."

"Exactly!" Weston smiled and moved the little ball with the tip of one finger. "The effect isn't really a space drive at all, it is more like recreating a duplicate of the original, then destroying the original."

"What!" Steve looked at the old man. "Destroying the original!"

"Yes. The difficult part is, of course, reproducing the identical wave-pattern which will force the electrons into the proper orbits. That merely duplicates whatever it is you are working with. Then, comes the focusing of the wave-pattern, and it's this which takes such an incredible amount of power and machinery! By some method, we are still trying to learn just how the guardians managed to focus the exact pattern of this ship at any point they wished. By some method, perhaps using other dimensions, they could focus that pattern even across the galaxy and do it without any obvious loss of time. The pattern focuses, the duplicate ship takes form, the Original is destroyed, and to an outside observer, or even to the crew themselves, the ship and contents have moved an incredible distance in a split second."

"I see," Steve said slowly, "but why wouldn't the drive work with men?"

"Remember the pattern must be exact. Every mote, molecule, atom and particle of atom must be in exactly the correct ratio to each other particle. No matter how carefully they aligned their machines, there must always be some margin of error. With robots and the more crude atomic structure of metal, this error doesn't matter. With men, it will be fatal. A misplaced neuron, and a man would have lost a degree of memory. A misplaced atom of the chemical structure of his body, and he would die from internal poisons. A slight inaccuracy of cell structure, and a man would become rotten with cancer: a monstrous freak, or a glandular idiot. The risks are terrible and will prevent men from ever using the instant-drive as it now is."

"Wait!" Steve stared at the old man a sudden hope burning deep within his cold eyes. "Must the entire ship be transmitted? Could you arrange the scanning machinery so as to send an object, say a nulgrav ship, rather than the entire vessel?"

"I don't know." Weston stared at the young man. "I can see no reason why it couldn't be done. Why?"

"If it can be done, then do it, and do it as soon as possible. I have a plan, and I know that we can beat the Vendians yet. Hurry, Weston. Get back to work and alter the machinery so as to send a nulgrav ship instead of this whole giant vessel."

He stared after the half running figure of the old man, then turned as Edwards entered the great chamber. The commander had rested a little, and his features had lost some of their previous strain. He grinned at Steve and hitched at his belt. "Look, Steve, I'm, not much use here, and I want to get back into space. Will you give me clearance for an armed nulgrav ship?"

"Where are you going?"

"Out to Sirius. I want to keep watch on those blue devils." He didn't sound any too hopeful that the young head of Planetoid Disposals Ltd. would grant his request. To his apparent surprise, Steve nodded.

"Very well. Jack, you may have a ship, but on one condition."

"Yes."

"That you stay well out of harm's way, and that you keep in constant sub-etheric radio contact with us here."

"I'll keep in contact, but why must I keep out of harm's way? I'd hoped to whittle the odds down a little, get a ship or two if possible. How can I do that if I'm afraid to venture too near?"

"Don't let's argue about it, Jack. If you don't want to go, then I'll send someone else. I want you to keep watch on Vendis for me—close watch. I want you to tell me when they seem about ready to blast from the planet—and Jack!"

"Yes?"

"When I order you to, I want you to engage the nulgrav drive and blast back to Earth. Do it and don't argue. Agreed?"

Slowly Edwards nodded and held out his hand.

CHAPTER THIRTEEN

Blue light streamed from the metal walls of the engine room of the great vessel, and sweating men laboured as they strove to adjust and align the great humped bulks of the electronic scanning machines. Within a cleared space in the centre of the room, the smooth hull and severe outlines of a small nulgrav ship rested on a cradle, and men carefully position the ship into delicate focus with the alien machines.

Steve stood watching the scene, his young features drawn and strained with fatigue and constant effort. He tried to smile down at the slender figure of Madge standing beside him, and with a worried expression, she looked up at him.

"Do you think that it will work, Steve?"

"It must work, dear; we have no time to try anything else." He glanced at the shimmering screen of the sub-etheric radio and frowned at the blank surface. Then he gestured towards the operator and shouted above the noise of clanging metal and labouring men: "What happened? I told you to retain constant contact."

"Yes, sir, but Commander Edwards broke contact."

"The fool!" Steve tightened his lips in anger. "Re-establish contact. Use emergency wave and attention signal. Let me know when he is on the screen!"

"Yes, sir."

"Edwards?" Madge frowned as she stared at the tall young man at her side. "Isn't he here with you?"

"No, dear, he took a ship and blasted towards Vendis, I told him to maintain constant contact with me, and he's disobeyed!"

"Is that so important?" She smiled a little at his worried expression. "Edwards knows what he is doing."

"Yes, but he doesn't know what I'm doing. I don't want him to be hurt."

"Hurt?" Madge laughed. "How can you touch him from here?"

Steve shrugged and watched a file of men enter the great chamber. They carried long bulky objects and treated those objects with exaggerated care. Carefully they entered the smooth hull of the nulgrav ship, and Madge tugged at his sleeve.

"Steve! What were those men carrying?"

"Atomic explosives," he said absently. "We should have a full load by now."

"Atomics?" She bit her lip as she stared at the glistening vessel. "Won't such a load injure the crew, cause radiation burns?"

"Perhaps." He was deliberately casual. "It won't matter though, there will only be one crew member, and he won't live long enough to worry about radiation sickness."

He stepped forward as the radio operator gestured towards him, the girl close behind. The lined face of Edwards limned itself on the screen, and Steve choked back the sarcastic words he had been about to utter at the sight of the distant commander's expression.

"Edwards! What's wrong?"

"Everything." Edwards wiped his stained face and neck. His hand came away wet with blood. "Steve! The blue devils are about to blast! I swept in as near as I could and managed to monitor one of their radio broadcasts. They have set zero-hour, and once they blast from the planet, nothing can stop them. Nothing!" He sounded almost hysterical.

"How much time do we have?"

"Not enough. They have set zero-hour for exactly ninety minutes of our time. Ninety minutes, Steve! After that, Earth and all the civilised worlds will be either conquered or destroyed."

"Where are you now?"

"About a quarter of a light-year from Vendis."

"Then retreat to a distance of a full light-year. Have your engines ready. Better set automatic controls activated by light pressure. I want you to scan the planet, relaying the vision over the sub-etheric radio, and it is important that you retreat at the speed of light when the critical moment comes."

"I don't understand?" The commander's face registered bewilderment. "What are you planning to do?"

"I'm going to destroy the planet. Now, follow my order. I'll explain everything later."

Steve turned from the screen and raced across the metal floor of the great room. Weston glanced up from where he worked at the sound of the young man's footsteps and irritably shook his head.

"Leave me alone, can't you? How can I be expected to work with these constant interruptions?"

"Listen, Weston. Hurry and prepare the ship for transit. I must leave within the hour, understand? Drop everything else and prepare the ship for transit."

"Are you insane? If I can't solve how to prevent the automatic dispersal of the original wave-pattern, you will die!"

"That doesn't matter—now."

Steve turned and bumped heavily into the slight figure of Madge. She stared at him, her features white and drawn, and with an odd choking sound buried her face against his chest.

"I knew it," she sobbed. "You're going to die, to kill yourself. Why, Steve? Why?"

"Someone must pilot the ship, Madge," he explained gently. "Our only chance is to crash through their protective barrier as fast as possible. I will materialise very near the planet, too near for their guarding vessels to destroy me. I shall activate the nul-grav screen and blast at full power towards Vendis. When the screen collapses, I shall use the ionic rockets. Whatever happens, it will be impossible to stop the ship, and it is loaded with enough atomic explosives to blast Vendis to dust, and all the ships of their fleet for a distance of a million miles. The war will be over, Madge, and mankind can work and live in peace again."

"But you will die!"

"Perhaps not. If Weston can control the automatic destruction of the original wave-pattern, then I will live. To you watching here, the nulgrav ship will remain as it is, nothing will have appeared to happen, but for a brief while there will be two ships, one here and one plunging down on Vendis. Two ships, Madge, and two crew members. I shall die on Vendis, but I will live here." He touched her gently on the chin. "Try and imagine it, dear. I shall not be in two places at once, it isn't like that at all. A duplicate of me will pilot a duplicate of the nulgrav ship. The duplicates will perish, but the originals will remain."

He did not think it worthwhile to tell her of the old scientist's doubts as to the possibility of retaining the original.

An alarm bell rang, and an orderly raced up to Steve.

"Zero-hour, sir. Commander Edwards reports that the enemy fleet is preparing to blast!"

Gently Steve kissed the girl on her upturned lips, then without a backward glance ran towards the smooth hull of the waiting vessel. Metal clanged behind him, and with hands which trembled a little, he strapped himself into the padded chair before the controls. A screen flashed into life beside him.

"Ready?" Weston looked anxious and drawn.

"Ready." Steve smiled at the old man and half raised his hand in farewell. The screen went dark and, for a moment, tension gripped the waiting man.

Slowly, gently, as if time had lengthened and sensation increased to a fantastic degree, strain began to make itself felt. Strange energies laved him, penetrating the metal of the hull, the stored atomics, the flesh and brain of the solitary man; energies probing to the very core of the atomic structure of ship and man. The energies of the scanning machines.

Things seemed to grow a little unreal. Stars blazed against the smooth plastic of the instrument panel. Eddies of motion disturbed the motionless vessel. Steve felt a splitting, a separating, a dream-like sense of duel identity, and for a moment, panic sent the blood pounding through his arteries.

Tensely he sat waiting, not resisting the strange throb of alien energies, but forcing himself to remain calm, his mind alert. Suddenly agony lanced through him, a fierce stabbing in each and every cell of his quivering body. His vision blurred, the instrument panel swirled in a soft greyness, the round discs of the dials before him distorted, becoming oval, then square, and finally vaporous spheres of coiling grey mist.

* * * *

The pain returned, sickening pain, as if he were being torn apart, as if every atom of his quivering body had been split and halved with knives of white-hot metal. He gripped the controls, the sweat starting from every pore of his trembling body. He screamed, the sound echoing flatly from the swirling mist around him. He screamed and screamed and—

Stars blazed before him. Huge brilliant stars, the great suns of the Sirian cluster. Automatically, not fully realising what he did, he pressed the firing levers of the ship, engaged the nulgrav drive, and sped towards a section of the heavens in which a small world spun slowly on its tilted axis.

He vomited, a warm gush of sticky red fluid staining the front of his uniform. He tried to wipe it away and stared in horror at his scaled and rotting skin. He touched his face and felt the bumps and warts of cancer blossoming around his eyes and mouth. He vomited again, and with a peculiar sense of relief, knew that he was dying.

Something smashed against the hull, and with a screaming of released energy, the nulgrav field collapsed and filled the vessel with the acrid stench of burning insulating and charred metal. Grimly, he pressed down on the firing levers, sending the vessel plunging ever nearer to the slowly spinning world which was his target.

He sagged in his chair, agony lancing through him, staining the clean plastic of the panel with ugly stains of blood and vomited slime. He fought for breath as the acceleration pressed against his almost useless lungs, and dully he felt the fresh pain of broken ribs stabbing into his internal tissue.

"For Earth!" he muttered and tried to grin. "For Earth!"

Abruptly the muffled thunder of the rockets died. The lights died; the instruments, every machine and surge of power, all died. The null-electronic field dragged at the ship, tried to halt its mad progress, tried, and failed. At a speed almost that of light itself, the ship swept through the barrier and suddenly the rockets thundered to fresh life.

A planet swirled before him, a world of brown earth and blue seas, a planet of ice and snow, warmth and life. Vendis! Home of the conquest-hungry blue-skinned people. Home of hate and destruction, planet of greed and war.

Steve stared down at it with dull and blurring eyes. His hands rested carelessly on the controls, his blood seeped from his lacerated body, and dully he wondered whether he would die before impact, or not. It didn't really matter. Nothing mattered now, nothing at all.

"Madge!" he breathed as the brown earth swept nearer. "Goodbye, Madge!"

Atmosphere whined around the ship, screaming at the smooth hull, and yet not even warming it so great was the speed of its passage. A city seemed to lie below, then it veered a little, and the ship plunged directly towards a great apron of concrete lined with the glittering hulls of many ships.

"For Earth!" the thing at the controls of the plunging ship mouthed and tried to smile. "For Earth!"

Brown dirt flowed like mud beneath the impact. Earth, then rock, both splashing from the force of the impact, splashing like water, tossed high into the air and marking the point of landing with a tremendous crater of riven stone.

Fire spread from the smashed vessel. Blue-white atomic flame. It spread, gushed, smashed aside dirt and stone in the terrible heat and speed of its ravening birth. Deep into the planet it thrust with its probing fingers of utter destruction. Delicate internal stresses were released, long slumbering fires awakened, the fury of the atomic explosion disturbed the equilibrium of the planet, and then—

Vendis burst open like a rotten fruit!

Energy washed for a million miles into space. Atomic disruption, searing ships and men in all directions, sterilising the entire area with a blazing wave of blasting destruction. Ships flared like moths caught in a flame, crisping and turning into molten blobs of steel and alloy. When the explosion wave had passed, Vendis and all it had stood for, had gone like a fragment of some evil dream.

* * * *

Steve shook his head in bewilderment as he stared at the controls. He swayed a little in the cushioned pilot's chair and passed trembling hands before his eyes. They were whole, the scarred and scaly skin had vanished—gone like the pain-racked lungs, and the blossoms of cancer around his eyes and mouth. Startled, he glanced at the flickering screen to his right.

"Steve! Answer me, man! Steve, are you all right?" Weston stared at him, his old thin face lined with worry. Steve smiled and began to unstrap himself from the padded chair. He trembled a little with reaction, and his hands fumbled at the buckles. Finally, they came free and he staggered out of the ship into the cleared area. Madge ran to meet him.

"Steve, oh Steve, for a moment I thought that you were dead!"

"What happened?" He stared at Weston, and the old scientist shook his head.

"I don't know, at least I don't know everything. I managed to heterodyne the automatic disruption machines; the original pattern, you, remained whole after the duplicates had been made;

but you were like a dead man, you wouldn't answer me, you sat like a thing of stone, like a dead man. What happened, Steve?"

"You made two bodies, Weston, but you couldn't make two egos. Even though I had a duplicate, I only had one intelligence for the both of them."

Steve shuddered slightly.

"I was with the duplicate, and it was horrible. I was dying, but I had expected that. What upset me was the manner of my death. I was a monstrosity, a diseased and rotting caricature of a man. I didn't think of the original pattern; I didn't think of anything but the necessity of destroying Vendis. I remember the moment of impact, then of course my duplicate body died, freeing my intelligence to return to its original home." He glanced at the assembled men standing around him. "Did I destroy Vendis, or was that all part of a dream also?"

"Vendis has been destroyed." Madge stirred in his arms. "Edwards approached far closer than you ordered him to. He watched the entire thing and relayed it back to us by sub-etheric impulse. Vendis is gone, Steve. You can rest now."

Something in her voice made him step back and glance at her sharply. Then understanding, he smiled.

"I know of what you are thinking, Madge. You are thinking that it is a terrible thing to destroy a world, but let me remind you of our charter, the charter of Planetoid Disposals Ltd."

He began to quote from memory:

"This franchise has been granted on the understanding that the company will at all times strive to clear the space lanes from all things harmful to the welfare of men and civilised peoples. They shall do what they think best to dispose, destroy, or render harmless all such menaces to be found in space, and at all times to hold themselves at the disposal of the World Government of Federated Man.

"You see, Madge? 'All things harmful', and the Vendians were surely that." He smiled at her and held out his arms. "Who else could have done what had to be done, except us? A planet had to be disposed of, and Planetoid Disposals Ltd. were the obvious people to do it."

"Forgive me, dear," she whispered. "I—"

The rest of her words were muffled against his lips as he swept her close.